LANDS END

An URSULA NORDSTROM Book

Also by Mary Stolz

Drawings by Dennis Hermanson

LANDS END
By Mary Stolz

Harper & Row, Publishers

New York   Evanston   San Francisco   London

This is for
Michael and Neil and Drayton
for Fran and Tommy
for Joani and Kristin and Lasse
for Lily and Fred
and for
Lands End

LANDS END

1

Although he'd been instructed, a lot more than once, not to go into his father's study when the door was closed and his father was—studying, or whatever, Josh thought, people did when they went into a room they called a study and closed the door—Joshua Redmond once again burst into his father's silence without knocking.

"Dad, do you know why dinosaurs were so stupid? I mean, it wasn't really their own fault at all, did you know that? It was because they had such very little heads. They had these great big enormous bodies and these little teeny heads. A dinosaur's body could be up to its neck in quicksand before the head caught on to what was up. By then it was too late to get the old corpus out. Usually. That's why their bones are found in layers of mud that's turned to rock."

This information was partly from the *Encyclopædia Britannica*, which Josh had undertaken to read straight through, partly from other reading, and partly his own interpretation. Josh liked to form his own interpretations. Sticking close to the facts, of course, but not so close that he felt crowded.

He could picture the huge beast, head like a bean balanced on a football, lumbering dimly into a marsh, legs lifting and descending with slow, enormous sounds of squashing, great tail dragging with a heavy sideways motion, and all of this feebly thinking bigness going steadily, steadily down, past any return to hard land, until only the little head, with popping eyes and wide-open mouth letting out a tinny scream, was left, and then that too would be gone. And years and years, millions, maybe billions, of them later, somebody poking around in the marsh that had now become rock would come across a bone, a tooth, and that was what was left of his dinosaur.

"Dinosaurs," he was going on, "were herbivores, practically all of them. Herbivores are animals that subsist mainly on herbage, and what happened was—"

His voice trailed off as he realized that his father was not listening. Only staring at him very hard.

"What's the problem?" Josh asked warily.

"The problem. You ask what the problem is."

"Well, yeah. I mean—"

"The problem. Well, let me see if I can state it once

again. The problem, Joshua, is how we are ever going to teach you not to walk into a room talking. Particularly if the room you've walked into had a closed door, meant for knocking upon."

"But, Dad, listen—"

"You listen. For a change. If your mother and I have asked you once we've asked you—I can't begin to estimate how many times—to find out if somebody else is saying something before you burst into a room with your tongue wagging. I could hear you all the way down the hall, talk, talk, talking as you came."

Josh hovered in the doorway, shifting from one foot to the other. "Yeah, but look—how could you be talking to someone? You're all alone in here."

"I was."

"That's what I said. So how could you be—"

"Suppose I hadn't been? With your own voice in your ears how can you hear other voices? Suppose your mother and I, or a friend, had been here discussing—"

"Mom's in the kitchen. Fixing chicken. We're going to have chicken for dinner. Again. With snook running all over the place. You want to go fishing, Dad?" At his father's expression, Josh lifted his shoulders, let them fall. "Anyway, you couldn't have any friend here because nobody's car is outside. Except ours, I mean—"

"You did not *know* I was alone. You were talking as you came. And you failed to knock on the door. Suppose I'd been pursuing an important thought? Suppose—" Mr. Redmond closed his eyes briefly, opened them and looked at the ceiling. "Maybe it's hopeless. Maybe you're a talking machine, and you'll go on talking with no thought for anyone else all the rest of your life, and we're just wasting our breath trying to teach you."

"Teach me what?"

"Manners, Joshua. Consideration for other people's feelings, for their privacy. Minor matters like that."

What Josh figured he hated more than anything else was the—the *mocking* tone that got into people's voices when they spoke to him. He couldn't believe it was because he talked a lot. To begin with, the things he was telling them were interesting. Besides, most of the time they—his parents, anyway—weren't saying anything anyway. His mother and father could go hours without saying a word. Not being angry or anything. They just didn't seem to have anything to say. Somebody had to talk.

Now, interrupted in the middle of his dinosaur statistics, Josh got this peculiar feeling inside him, as if his chest was suddenly too small for real breathing. It seemed that no matter where he went or whom he was with, people were mainly interested in shutting him up, and not at all interested in all the things he had to share and discuss.

He turned and started out of the room.

"Just a moment, Josh."

Joshua turned back to his father.

"What do you think you're doing now?" Mr. Redmond asked.

Josh shrugged.

"It is not courteous to walk out of a room without saying good-bye. Do you suppose you're ever going to acquire manners of any kind?"

Josh considered.

Not mannerly to walk into a room talking. Not courteous to walk out of it not talking. Were manners really more important than facts, than sharing all the stuff you learned? Probably. He glanced at his father, who was looking at him in a puzzled way.

"What's the matter with you, Joshua? Why are you just standing there, not saying anything?"

Boy, are they ever hard to please, thought Josh. A marvelous notion developed in his head. He opened his mouth to communicate this revolutionary idea to his father, quickly closed it again.

"Well? Well? What were you going to say?"

Josh shook his head. As a compromise toward not leaving a room without saying good-bye, he wiggled a hand, then turned and ran down the hall and up the stairs to his own room, where he closed the door and sat on the window seat, brooding.

All this store of lore he had. Just about everything man had ever learned from A to D, and now everyone was tired of listening before he'd even got to E. Well, he'd show them.

He got up and took a sheet of paper from a drawing pad he'd got for Christmas and never used, and a green felt-tipped pen.

Down there, in the stupid study, he'd begun to get this super idea. You couldn't make them pay attention to you if you talked. But what about if you didn't talk? Then what, huh?

The thing was, could he carry through? Lots of times he found himself saying something before he'd quite figured out what the point was, or if there was a point, or even if there was, just at that time, anything he especially wanted to say. Like the time he'd told them about dentistry all through dinner. He'd got sort of tired of it himself. Even the encyclopedia couldn't make dentistry grab you. Words like occlusion and caries and orthodontia couldn't carry the whole weight. Besides, he'd got the facts—there'd been an awful lot of them—muddled, and his father had told him so. In that way he had of telling somebody so.

"If you're going to give us an oral report on the oral cavity," Mr. Redmond had said, "at least have your information accurate. 'Caries' refers to decay, not to the condition of the bite."

"Whatever it refers to," his mother had said, "it is not dinner-table conversation."

That had done it for Dentistry. What came after that,

in the encyclopedia, was some enlightenment about a couple of places called Denton. Curious as he was about practically everything, Josh could not work up any steam about the Dentons.

The thing was—could he carry through on this idea? Sometimes he'd hear his own voice going on and on, like a top that wouldn't wind down, and all the while he was making up his mind to stop, he'd keep finding just one more thing that had to be said. And if somebody else was talking, he had to admit that most of the time he didn't listen as attentively as he should. Mostly he planned what to say when he interrupted them.

"So I talk too much," he muttered to himself. "So they're bored listening to me. I'll show them."

With the green pen, he wrote in capital letters,

I AM NOT GOING TO TALK
ANYMORE, SO NOBODY
TALK TO ME BECAUSE I
WON'T ANSWER.

The next thing was, where to put the sign. On his door? It might be ages before either of them came to look for him and saw it. Hang it on a string around his neck and walk around the house until they noticed and read it? He shook his head. That'd be childish.

On the bulletin board in the kitchen. That's where he'd put it. They all looked at the bulletin board. When they went into the kitchen it was the first place they looked, to see if there were any messages, or clippings from the newspaper, or if somebody had added a new cartoon.

Last week his father had put one up with a woman saying to a man, "Well, that's enough about me, let's talk about you. What did *you* think of my latest book?"

Mrs. Redmond had glanced at it and then said to her husband that he was antifeminist.

"Let's say anti-humanbeingist," Mr. Redmond had replied.

"What's the matter with human beings?" Josh asked.

"Just about everything. Most of them are so insecure you want to hit them, or else self-dramatizing egomaniacs, some of whom will probably be responsible for finishing off this planet. Not that it will leave any great gap in the galaxy."

Mr. Redmond often spoke this way, but Josh wasn't sure how much of it he actually meant. "What I mean is," he'd said to his father one day, "if you believe all that stuff, why're you usually in a pretty good mood?"

"Maybe because I believe it." At Josh's puzzled expression, Mr. Redmond had added, "Anyway, I'm usually only in a good mood in the morning. As the day goes on, I snap out of it."

Josh had laughed, but hadn't felt any closer to understanding what it was his father did believe.

He turned his mind back to the matter of his declaration. The bulletin board it was. He stomped down to the kitchen, where by good luck he found both of them, his mother still doing something with the chicken, his father staring out the window at his sloop, *Candide*. He couldn't sail her because last week in a high wind one of the spreaders had snapped and wasn't repaired yet. Mr. Redmond was a ship's chandler. His company outfitted freighters, oilers, tankers, with everything from hawsers to teaspoons. He was a man who liked his job and spent long hours at it. But what he loved was sailboats. What he loved was going out on the Gulf, by himself, on *Candide*. Mrs. Redmond wasn't much of a sailor and rarely went out. Josh went pretty often with his father. But they all knew he was happiest sailing alone, and Joshua couldn't figure it out. Not that sailing wasn't the greatest, and Josh usually went alone on his own little Sunfish, *Scorch*, but that was because there were so few kids at this end of the island. He wasn't alone by choice, as his father so often was.

His parents looked around and watched while Josh thumbtacked his notice to the board. It was so big it covered the cartoon and a column by Art Buchwald and a postcard from Chile from somebody they knew who was in Chile.

His father and mother looked at the announcement and exchanged glances. Josh detected a slight smile on his mother's mouth, but his father, as usual, went on looking as usual.

"Very good," said Mr. Redmond after a moment. "Have you set yourself a time limit to this stint, Josh?"

Josh started to shake his head, then refrained.

"You mean you won't even nod or shake your head?" his mother asked. "What if I really need an answer to something?"

He stood stolidly, staring at them, his lips compressed.

"Can't talk, and can't hear either," said Mr. Redmond. "Who'd ever have thought the day would come?"

Josh turned, went out the door, letting it slam behind him. His bike was leaning against the garage and he was on it and moving before Mrs. Redmond could do more than call after him.

"Josh? Josh, come back this moment and tell us where you're going! Josh, when will you be back?"

Joshua was into the street and away.

2

Pedaling along, the warm breeze in his face, he began to feel calmer. Sort of peaceful.

Except that he'd never seen any snow, he liked where he lived—on a long thin island, called a key, that had the Gulf of Mexico on one side and a bay on the other, and was still, at his end of the island, wild enough, with palm groves and mangrove swamps and Australian pines and miles of fine sand beach and sea oats and sea grapes. Though it was not the way it had been when his father had been a boy, it was still, to Josh, a great place to live.

The fishing wasn't what it had been in his father's boyhood, but you could still get sea trout and sheepshead and redfish and snook when they were running. You could get mullet with a gig or a net. There were

11

plenty of clams and crabs, if you took the trouble to go after them, and Josh frequently did. There were all kinds of birds. Herons and cormorants, egrets and owls, thrashers and kingfishers, flickers, mockingbirds, and towhees—hundreds of birds. And out on the water, when he sailed with his father on *Candide*, porpoises would come swimming a few feet away, diving, sloping in gray and glistening curves, making their strange grunting-singing sound as they raced or lazed past.

His parents owned about twenty acres at the tip of the island. They called their property Lands End. ("Without," Mr. Redmond would insist, "an apostrophe." "Why without an apostrophe?" "I don't know why. My father named it. Maybe he couldn't spell.")

Mr. Redmond said he meant to keep at least these twenty acres untouched, unviolated, unpolluted, un-built-upon, un-butted-in-upon. Of course, with motels and condominiums going up down all the rest of the key, they couldn't really keep their bit pure and apart. Already thousands of acres of mangrove swamp and palm groves had been ravaged, obliterated, destroyed forever by the builders, whose money, said Mr. Redmond, could buy anything, including the life of the land. He said that with construction going on at the rate it was, one day the whole island would simply sink beneath the water. He said that even if it meant losing his own part, he'd be glad enough to see it happen.

"Serve them right," he'd mutter.

"Serve who right, Dad?"

"All the island people who've sold out to those jackals, the developers."

"But if they've sold out, they probably aren't here anymore," Josh had once pointed out. "So it isn't going to serve them right. It's just going to sink us."

Mr. Redmond had scowled and not replied.

Some people hated the island, especially in summer, when the heat was often like a wet spinnaker collapsing on the land, or else it was so baked and sun-scorched that people fled into the cold, dead air conditioning of shops and houses and wouldn't stir out until dusk. The Redmonds did not have air conditioning in their house. Mr. Redmond said it was unnatural, Mrs. Redmond said it was unhealthy, and Josh just didn't like it.

Joshua Redmond, brown, barefooted, lover of water and shellfish, observer of birds and porpoises, liked the island just fine, in any weather, at any time of year. He liked the spring, when old sea-grape leaves littered the sandy yard and the new leaves appeared, coppery and glistening and almost transparent, and everywhere—perched on telephone wires or in hibiscus bushes or traveler's palms or pine boughs—the mockingbirds sang their clear and complicated song. He liked the heavy heat of summer, the storms of autumn, the crispness of winter. He couldn't be sure, because he hadn't been anywhere else, but he thought that surely nowhere else were there trees like the island trees. Mysterious banyans, stately golden shower trees and Australian pines, papayas and citrus trees and avocados and mangoes, and leaning palms that made a sound like rain when their great fronds moved in the wind. But mostly he loved the sea all around them, sometimes raging as if it would engulf the island, sometimes flat as a dish, sometimes arranged in tidy little waves as far as you could see.

He loved, as if it were his own and in need of his protection, little Catfish Island, out on the bay. No one, especially in summer, ever seemed to go there except himself, or once in a while Hank Burroughs or Clooney Powers with him. Mostly he went alone, sailing his Sunfish, *Scorch*, or paddling the canoe on windless days, pulling his boat well ashore before he left it to walk on ground spongy with pine needles, in the strangely, almost spookily, quiet air that always lay over Catfish Island.

When he was angry, which was pretty often, Catfish Island was where he went, the way some people, he supposed, went to friends or to the movies or for walks, or whatever other people did to recover from the sick, seething feeling of rage.

The moment he was either in the canoe or on *Scorch*, heading for the island, he could feel his anger going, like sea-foam disappearing into sand.

He'd beach his boat on the near side and then walk through the woods to the far side. If the tide was low enough, sometimes he'd lie out on the flats in shallow water, on an old surfboard he left there for the purpose. He'd lie so still that after a while small fish—mosquito fish and minnows—would begin to nibble at him. Once

14

he had stayed so still for so long that a conch, inching along at about an inch an hour, had finally made it to his side and pressed its ugly sucking foot against his leg, and then its fleshy mouth. Josh had gently detached it and sent it on its way, thinking, as he'd thought before, how strange a thing a conch was—so beautiful outside, so downright hideous inside. Still, it was one of nature's harmless creatures, and no threat to the builders as they were to it.

If the tide was up, he'd cast for a while, not caring if he caught anything and usually throwing a catch back if it hadn't taken the hook too hard. A tussle with a ladyfish, that bony, slender, pretty fighter, would melt anyone's rage, in Josh's opinion. An hour or two on the island, a glimpse of the barn owl that lived there flying silently overhead, or of a long-legged raccoon going quickly down the beach, was enough to make a person forget, for a while, his own personal sense of importance.

For his age, which was sort of twelve, Joshua Redmond could be detached about himself sometimes. He wished in a way that things could've been different. He wished he'd had some brothers, or even only one. He wished he didn't so often feel that he got in his parents' way. But, looking at other kids, he guessed he didn't have it so bad.

Hank Burroughs came pedaling in the other direction, and they slowed as they spied each other.

"Hey, Josh, what's new?" said Hank, adding hastily, "Don't tell me everything. Just the bare bones."

Josh scowled and pushed off.

Even bigmouth Burroughs. Everybody. All of them. Family, friends, teachers. All down on him for talking. Well, they'll find out, he muttered to himself. They'll find out, he vowed, detachment slipping away. Maybe he'd never say anything again in his whole life. He could picture how, after a few days, his mother and father would be pleading with him, begging for just one word.

"We don't care how much you talk," his mother would say, beseeching, holding his hand in hers, tears pouring up and down her face. "Please, dear Josh, talk as much as you want, but just be the way you used to be."

And his father. "*Say* something, Joshua." Beseeching even harder. "Say anything. Just *talk* to us again."

The picture of his father beseeching wouldn't entirely jell. Still, just thinking about it made Josh feel better. He stopped, one foot on the ground, to watch a flock of low-flying pelicans. Most birds flew with their heads stretched forward, but pelicans, with their heads upright, looked like little Viking ships as they calmly sailed the air. Josh, who tended to set himself improbable and unnecessary choices, wondered now and then what he would do, given the option of pelicans or porpoises. They were both such great creatures, he didn't see how to do without either, and sometimes got

16

pretty exercised trying to decide between them before he remembered that he didn't have to. Not, anyway, for a while yet. His father said that with the way things were going, if madmen didn't finish off the world, then fools would.

"Here," he'd said the other day, shaking the newspaper as if it were infected, "they've appropriated another few paltry million for flood relief, and a few billion for seeing to it that the country gets so paved over that the second deluge is practically assured. Too many people, too many automobiles, too many motor courts and potato chips and parking lots and shopping centers—"

Josh, wondering how potato chips had got on the list, decided it was because his father had a notion that potato chips were kid stuff and so to be disapproved of. Josh suspected that his father wasn't entirely pleased about the existence of children. Including his own one son. Not that he really believed that. But not that he really didn't believe it, either. His father could be swell, patient about explaining things, provided Josh would listen without interrupting. He turned up at parents' meetings at school. He took Josh sailing with him—and his wife, if she'd go. Every year, almost, he took them on some sort of vacation somewhere. The ships chandlery, about twenty miles away in town, kept Mr. Redmond busy, but when he wasn't there or out on the Gulf in *Candide*, he was with his family. Not like Hank's father, who

17

traveled in pharmaceuticals and was away a lot, and was drunk most of the time when he was home. But Mr. Burroughs never seemed to mind how many kids Hank had hanging around the house, how many bikes were parked in the driveway, how many bags of potato chips and bottles of pop got used up.

Well, he wouldn't, thought Josh, want Mr. Burroughs for a father, either. He thought that over, and nervously tried to erase the *either* from his mind.

But about pelicans and porpoises—his father said that one day they'd be gone from the island and the waters around the island because of what men considered the prior interests of men—in this instance, housing and commerce. Everybody, these days, was making a buck on condominiums, he said, which gave pelicans and porpoises, which were not marketable, a dim prospect. Josh could only hope it wasn't so. His father could be wrong, or things could change, people might catch on in time to what they were doing. Maybe everything was going to turn out all right for the porpoises and pelicans.

It was Josh's nature—despite his fits of fury—to look on the cheery, hopeful side. If there didn't, in some cases, seem to be such a side, he made one up.

Idly he pushed on, passing the house nearest theirs, a half mile down toward the village. A big stucco thing that had once been washed a sort of pale lemon color but was now just streaky and faded and rusty near the drains and gutters. It had a black cast-iron gate in the high stucco wall facing the street. It had an iron gate inside, too, between the big entry hall and the living room. It was a huge house, and awful.

The Redmonds' house was wooden and low and old and weathered, and was marvelously kept, as Josh's mother was a famous good housekeeper and his father a nut for neatness. The windows always sparkled, and in front they had some beautiful bushes and trees—gardenia and hibiscus and Brazilian pepper and avocado and lemon trees and a fine traveler's palm, and a tremendous ancient banyan that people sometimes stopped their cars to look at. At the back of the house a long wooden dock ran out into the bay. Mr. Redmond kept *Candide* moored quite far out, in deep water, although years before, when *his* father had built the house, he'd docked it right at the pier where they now kept the skiff. That had been before the U. S. Army Corps of Engineers had, for reasons never made clear to anyone on the island, built a breakwater just north of them. It had changed the tide patterns so much that the harbor had silted up, and what had been deep water beneath their dock was now shallow even at high tide. Mr. Redmond wouldn't take *Candide* down the bay at all, and hadn't for years because he said the sands shifted so rapidly and strangely that you couldn't even trust the channel markers.

Candide had a fin keel and so had to be kept moored, but Josh's little Sunfish, with the centerboard out, was kept pulled up on the sand near the house, along with the canoe. Mast and sail were stored on the back porch along with fishing gear, mullet nets, paddles, crab nets, boat cushions, a big basket of shells that Josh had collected and not got around yet to sorting, some nice pieces of driftwood, and a whole lot of other stuff, all of it with a place to go and all of it kept in its place.

But this house, this place that Mr. Redmond called Tincture of Spain, was run-down and tacky, for all it had been, not too many years before, pretty imposing. When Senator Freebee had owned it. Now the windows were cracked and dirty, the front yard full of sand and crabgrass and dead bushes. Josh hated the place, because of Senator Freebee.

He slowed, and stopped, regarding the place curiously. Somebody was doing something to it. There were workmen raking the yard, cleaning the windows, and carting out junky-looking furniture to a van pulled up under the porte cochere. Or carting it *in?* They seemed to be taking it in. A big old sofa with stuff coming out of the arms, a table that looked like a beat-up door with dingy brass legs, a chest of some kind with chips and stains all over the wood. Was somebody going to turn the place into a secondhand shop? The people around here would have conniptions. And why bother to clean the windows if you were going to load the place up with rubble and refuse? Like that sofa there, and those raggedy armchairs.

Tincture of Spain hadn't been lived in for several years, not since Mr. Freebee, who'd been a state senator, had been found hanging from a beam in the living room, having used a big stepladder to get himself and the noose up that high. Senator Freebee had disgraced his office doing something financial and had gotten caught, and had taken, people said, "the coward's way out." Josh didn't see how you could call hanging yourself from a beam in your living room cowardly. He thought it was grisly but brave. But although plenty of people had found it exciting to talk about, the whole business gave Josh the creeps, and whenever anyone got on the subject, he walked away.

Death, dying, the whole business was uncheerful, and he didn't want to talk about it or think about it. Especially not somebody dead whom he'd known walking around and talking just like everybody else. Not that he had known Senator Freebee well, since he'd usually been in the state capital attending to the state's business —or, as it turned out, giving the state the business. He'd taken bribes, or given bribes, or something. Anyway, the senator had not been around much even when he was alive, but he was somebody they'd all seen and known; they'd known Mrs. Freebee too and Josh had gone to school with the Freebee kids—who were older than he was, but still, they were there. After the senator had been found and cut down, and the newspapers, excited as the kids at school, had written about it, Mrs. Freebee and her three children had left town, left the state, maybe left the country, to put it all behind them.

Josh, who hadn't known any of them particularly well, felt uneasily sorry for the family; but he hated the dead senator, who'd done such a mangy thing only half a mile from his neighbors, the Redmonds. Josh had had nightmares about it for a year.

So now, it seemed, somebody without much money was moving into the Freebee house, and the ghost, if there was a ghost, of the senator who hadn't minded sinning but had minded very much getting caught, would be turfed out for good. Josh was pleased.

He leaned his bike against a tree and went forward to find out what was up. Going through the iron gates, open today though they'd been closed for years, he found Fat Matt, one of the park guards, standing at the door.

"Hey there, Josh," he said cheerfully. "What d'ya thinka this, huh? New zoo vet and his family moving in. Looks like they've been boardin' the animals, don't it?" He waved a hand toward the moving men. "Must be a passel of 'em. I've already counted six beds—one's a double—and a crib. Lemme tell you, the best-looking stuff goin' in there's been the packing crates, and they belong to the moving company. Hey, you there!" One of the men had dropped a box, and Fat Matt advanced upon him, Authority protecting the interests

22

of the new veterinarian—who, Josh supposed, would be, like Fat Matt himself, a Park and Zoo employee, and therefore a fellow worker.

Spared the necessity of deciding, just now, whether not talking went only for his family, or for everyone else too, Josh mounted his bike and pedaled toward the park.

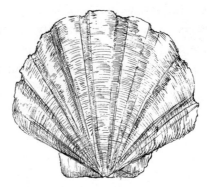

3

Once there, he was obliged to decide all over again, and quickly at that. He was getting hungry, and as he passed an ice-cream-and-hot-dog wagon, he pulled up and got off his bicycle.

There were several people waiting to be served, but finally the man indicated him and said, "What'll it be, young fellow?"

Josh had to make up his mind. Did this not-talking go only for his father and mother, or for everybody? In other words, was he not-talking, or wasn't he? He was. It went for everyone. As far as the world was concerned, Joshua Redmond had quit talking. Not only that, he'd quit hearing. Friends, family, teachers, cops, hot-dog men—they'd all just have to face it. Josh Redmond wasn't talking to them, and he wasn't hearing them.

He pointed toward the ice-cream bin.

"Okay, okay. What flavor?"

Josh continued to point into the bin. Then, remembering something he'd seen in a movie, he pointed to his mouth and shook his head.

"You mean you can't talk, kid?" said the man, sounding suspicious.

Josh pretended not to hear. He leaned over the bin and jabbed his finger toward an ice cream pop. He got out some money and held it forward, the right change, because someone his age, whether he could talk or hear or not, would know what an ice cream pop cost.

"Does he want the chocolate, do you think?" the hot-dog man said to a woman who was waiting with a couple of little children. A note of sympathy had come into his voice.

"Poor little fellow. Apparently he's deaf and dumb."

Josh listened happily to the kindness and concern in their voices.

"Why don't you show him each flavor and let him pick?" said the woman.

Josh took a strawberry and again extended his hand with the money in it toward the vendor.

"Oh, don't charge the poor thing," said the woman. "How can you take money from a child who's deaf and dumb? I'll pay for him," she said, loudly generous.

Josh only just prevented himself from blurting, "Just because I'm deaf and dumb, lady, doesn't mean I'm a beggar." But he kept his mouth shut tight, since he wasn't supposed to know what she was saying. He continued to push his money at the hot-dog man, who smiled and patted him on the head as if Josh were six.

"I'd better take it," he said to the woman. "'Spect even a dummy's got pride, huh?"

Crimers, Josh said to himself, walking off, pushing his bike and moodily licking the ice cream stick. *Crimers*. Did being deaf and dumb make a guy a sponger, and only six years old? Did they think somebody deaf and dumb didn't have any self-respect?

He stopped by a bench, sat down, and stared at his shoes. Sometimes he was sort of tempted to agree with his father. People were cruddy. The only thing was, his father seemed to think that all the time, while Josh only thought so once in a while, when he was faced with somebody cruddy. That woman being twenty-five cents generous at the top of her lungs. The hot-dog guy calling him a dummy. Even if you thought somebody couldn't hear you, calling him a dummy was—cruddy.

People! he said to himself, and decided to bike on over to the zoo and look at animals.

He never could make up his mind if he loved the zoo or hated it. He loved animals. And here, in this zoo, they tried to give them some sort of freedom. Some of them, that was. The lions lay out on a kind of plain, surrounded by a deep moat, and there were no bars between them and the people looking at them. Lazy and tan and tame-seeming, the big cats stretched out in the shade of trees, glancing now and then without interest at peacocks moving among them. The peacocks dragged their heavy, bobbing tails that shimmered with color, and turned their tiny crowned heads in jerky motions from side to side.

And in another part of the zoo, on an island in a man-made lake, there were flamingos, gawky and beautiful, with rose-colored plumage. They moved about their island, twining their snaky necks in queer patterns, beating their huge wings, looking sort of like dancers. Even at mating time, when the males fought, there was something sort of dancy about their battles. They looked free enough, the flamingos. As if they could fly off any time they chose, but just chose to remain here. The thing was—they were not free. They all had their wings clipped. They'd been pinioned, so no matter how winged and wild they looked, they were, really, cripples. Josh compared them unfavorably (unfairly, he knew) to the birds of sea and shore, the free wild birds that came and went, even visiting this lake when they wished and leaving when they wished. It wasn't the flamingos' fault that they were in such a fix, but Josh didn't really like them.

The big cats, except the lions, were caged. Every time Josh stopped to look at them, he wished he could somehow let them free. The tigers, the biggest of all, seemed to him to be indifferent, as if they had somehow risen above captivity, above the people who'd encaged them. But the leopards and jaguars had a—a bitter look.

"Unresigned," his father had said, one time when the Redmonds had come over here for a look at some new baby lions. Like Josh, Mr. Redmond liked animals very much. He wouldn't allow pets. Josh had never had a dog or a cat, and he guessed he'd have to grow up before he got one. His father didn't approve of what he called the dog's "slave mentality," and cats killed birds.

His father did not like the zoo, and had only gone that day because it was Josh's birthday and Josh had asked because of the lion cubs. That had been a couple of years ago, and he was just as glad his father had never come with him again. The kind of information Mr. Redmond handed out on a trip to practically anywhere was almost sure to make a guy wish he'd stayed at home.

He remembered how the three of them had stopped in front of the cheetah enclosure and looked for a long time at the beautiful pair of cats wearing expressions of innocent alertness even here in jail.

"The cheetah," Mr. Redmond had said, "is a doomed species."

Joshua had stared intently at the two cats, with their long thin legs and lovely spotted fur and huge round eyes. Cheetahs had two black marks going down from the inside corners of their eyes to the sides of their mouths. They looked like the tracks of tears.

"Why?" he'd asked, wishing he wouldn't, but forced, somehow, as he often was with his father, to go into matters he'd have preferred to overlook.

"Mostly it comes of women wanting to wear their fur. Takes about seventeen of those to make one coat for one greedy woman. They use only the side pelts. And men or women, frantic to parade wealth, use hides like this to cover their car seats or their sofa cushions or their beds. Anything to make a display," his father had said.

"But—why do they have to get extinct?" Josh had persisted. "They could have babies here, like the lions. Living in a zoo isn't the greatest, I guess, but it's better than not living at all, not having any cheetahs in the world at all."

"Cheetahs will not breed in captivity. Never have been known to. Nope, they're finished." Mr. Redmond spoke in a dry, informative way, as if he didn't care one way or the other. It would take, Josh had thought, someone like me or Mom, who knows him, to know how much he minds. "They'd be safe enough," Mr. Redmond had gone on, "if they were ugly, like those peccaries over there. Anyway, safer. Nothing much in this world is safe as long as it contains human beings."

Somewhere in the zoo was a sign over a framed box. It said, *You Are Now Looking At The Most Dangerous Animal In The World.* When you walked over to see, you found yourself looking into a mirror. Did that teach anybody anything? Most of the people who looked just laughed and strolled off discarding cigarettes or candy wrappers. Only a few looked kind of thoughtful.

"Well," Mrs. Redmond had said, "at least the cheetahs don't know they're doomed. Maybe there's some sort of comfort in that."

And the three of them had looked at the cheetahs, sitting so straight, their shoulders touching as if for comfort. They didn't look doomed and certainly couldn't know they were, but they looked sad. Maybe it was just because of the way those dark tears that weren't really tears at all fell down their cheeks.

It hadn't been the best birthday ever, in spite of the three lion cubs who tumbled over the reclining body of their mother, tossed each other about in imitation battle, and abruptly flopped panting to the ground, resting their wide heads on huge paws and seeming to fall asleep in an instant.

The lions here had a kind of freedom and would breed in captivity. The cheetahs were caged and would not.

Sitting today in his self-imposed silence, thinking back to that birthday, Josh had a sense of understanding how his father felt about things. He wouldn't, himself, ever want to be like his father. Coldly angry once in a while but mainly good-humored because he really didn't give a damn. Maybe at one time his father had cared very much, as Josh cared now, about the world and the creatures in it and its chances of survival, but then when everything, in his view, had turned out so badly (the island despoiled in the name of business, the cheetahs doomed through greed) he'd just gone in the other direction, that of not caring at all.

This unexpected perception of his father's point of view seemed, to Josh, to make his own vow of silence just silly. Things were bad enough, probably, without a person going out of his way to make them worse. Anyway, the plain fact was he'd never be able to go on playing deaf and dumb to the world.

There was too much to say.

4

On the way back, he met Fat Matt trudging heavily toward the park. He stopped when he saw Josh, took off his cap, and wiped his sweaty forehead.

"Well, guess all their junk is in. Funny they wouldn't't've got one of them here to see to it themselves, except maybe they figure what the heck difference could it make, to which I say amen. All that busted-up stuff all the way from Cleveland—down here you couldn't even make a tag sale out of it. Dr. Claven said to just sort of get the right kind of stuff in the rooms, like don't put the dining-room table in the bedroom, and me and the movin' guys more or less doped it out, but you think of all that garbage bein' shipped clear from Ohio, it don't make sense. They coulda left it all and stopped down here to the Salvation Army and got as good or better. Good thing Dr. Claven arranged for the Park to rent that ol' cheat Freebee's house to them—all the kids they got they're gonna need room. When Doc Claven sees their *be*longin's he's gonna wonder why he went to the trouble of havin' the windows cleaned and the yard cleared out. I figure this bunch'll have the place back to ought in nothin' flat. What's the matter with you, Josh? Whyn't you say anything? You sick or something? Usually got a tongue waggin' like a pup's tail and I ain't heard a peep outa you today. Got this-here louryngitis or somethin'?"

Josh, wondering if it was at all possible that he sounded to other people the way Fat Matt sounded to him, sighed and said he'd been feeling poorly.

"Nothin' serious, I hope," said Fat Matt. "Well, I gotta be gettin' along, wasted the whole day here, not that Doc Claven can have any kick comin' seein' as how he sent me over here hisself to see to things, which I *done*."

"When are they coming? The new vet and his family?"

"*Quién sabe*, as they say down Mexico way. Pretty soon, I expect. They're drivin' from Ohio, where this new fellow, Dr. Arthur, was at the university there. Doc Claven seems pleased as punch to be gettin' him, appears he must be a pretty good vet all right, and Doc Claven sure could use some help, seein' he can't *ad*-ministrate and do all the animal doctorin' too, which he's *been* doin' ever since that squirt, Beldon, decided overnight to go into private practice. Can't blame him in a way, the kind of pay the zoo thinks ade*quate* to a person's needs, but I don't myself see how anyone who's worked with tigers can descend to pussycats and poodles, not that *they* aren't all right in their place, too. But I suppose Beldon'll make a packet out of it around here, all the rich b's we got in this area if you'll excuse the expression, but you'd think he coulda given somethin' more than a week's notice, wouldn't ya? Well, can't stand here gabbin', Josh. Gotta get back and quit for the day, hey?" He laughed with amusement at himself.

Josh, shaking his head, continued on home. *Did* he sound like that? If everybody either told him or somehow made it clear without telling him that he talked too much (and there was no if about it), then perhaps it was a fact. But the things *he* had to say and tell people were interesting. Not just a bunch of prattle like Fat Matt handed out. Except that it was plain Fat Matt found what he had to say interesting as all get-out. So if I, thought Josh, find what *I* have to say interesting as all get-out, could I still sound like Fat Matt to somebody listening to *me*?

It was a gruesome idea.

There was nobody home at his house. A note from his mother on the bulletin board under his announcement said that she'd gone to the market and would be back soon, but since he didn't know when she'd left, he didn't know when she'd be back.

He took an apple and wandered to the back of the house, where the living room was. With no surprise he saw the skiff tied up at the mooring and *Candide* gone. Right now his father was somewhere on the Gulf of Mexico, running before the wind. Josh figured there must be a good fifteen-knot wind. It was one of the best things in the world—to be under sail with a good breeze blowing. To port and starboard the waves would rise in two glassy wings, and the white wake would spread out like crocheting on the water, and the porpoises, swooping and sounding and reappearing, would bear you company.

His own Sunfish, *Scorch*, didn't leave enough wake to attract them, but sometimes when he was out in the bay (he wasn't allowed to take *Scorch* into the Gulf, and certainly not the canoe) he could see the porpoises curvetting after some big boat, and he'd idle along, just watching.

He wished his father had waited and taken him on *Candide*. His own fault, of course. All that about not talking. Only, out there on the water, with the waves swelling past, the wake churning and tossing, he usually fell silent anyway. He usually just listened to the wind in the stays, just watched the birds leaning into the wind. And his father, who could light a pipe in any wind, would lean back, gently moving the tiller, gently puffing on the pipe, and it seemed to Josh that it was the one time they could be together without that feeling of tension that seemed to vibrate between them so often once they were ashore again.

Maybe if a person could just stay out there on the water there wouldn't be any problems. You could just sail along, with the porpoises looping lazily beside you, and be free.

Of course, if you thought about it further, you weren't entirely free. Or you weren't if, like Josh's father, you refused to have a motor on your boat. Then you were in the wind's hands, in a way of speaking. No motor was why Mrs. Redmond so rarely sailed with them. She always had an appointment she had to keep without fail, and winds failed no matter who wanted to keep what; and when the wind failed you could drift for hours, going in slow circles, or going nowhere, like the sailors in *The Ancient Mariner*. Josh and his father had been becalmed plenty of times, and now and then had run aground on sandbars and had to wait for the next tide to take them off, or for somebody with a power boat to pull them off. Mrs. Redmond told her husband that if he'd get a motor, she'd go with them oftener.

"But I can't have a motor," he'd said.

"Why in the world not?"

"It's noisy. It's—not sailing. Sailing is sailing. With sails, with the wind, with your eye and your hand and a tiller. Motoring is something, I suppose, but it is *not* sailing."

Josh agreed with his father. Put a motor on a sailboat and it wasn't really a sailboat anymore. It was a power boat with sails on it. If you could always switch to power in a pinch, he thought, you would lose your feeling for the wind, for the way the sails felt. Skimming along with his father, who often let him take the tiller, Josh knew you got to feel how the wind was going to take the sails a moment before it did. And just that moment made the difference between sailing a boat and sailing a boat with a motor on it.

He went to get the mast for *Scorch* off the back porch, stopped to watch a little blue heron come along the jetty, stepping carefully as if fearful for the safety of his skinny, fragile legs. He turned his thin, long neck slowly from side to side, so as to tip each eye down, examining the wood for grubs—of which there must've been lots, because every few seconds he thrust his needly beak into the wood and came up with something sizeable that he'd gulp down, after which he'd stand for a moment as if to savor it, and then proceed as before. Josh watched lovingly. What thin birds they were, herons. Even the big ones—Ward's heron and the Florida heron—had legs and great long toes as thin as pipe cleaners and knee bones like finger knuckles. Unlike the sturdy pelicans, herons and egrets had a practically breakable look. Cormorants, who were slender all right, never seemed fragile. When they sat on the pilings, black against the sky, wings outspread to catch the sun to dry their feathers, they looked powerful and absolutely sure of themselves.

But whether they looked delicate or tough, most of the birds around here weren't fearful. You could be almost on top of a heron or an egret before it'd wing casually off. Unless they were being harassed by sea gulls, pelicans were positively friendly, congregating at the end of the dock and accepting from Josh's hand the leavings of fish he'd caught and filleted. And sea gulls were the sassiest of all. They'd strut around him on the dock while he cleaned his fish, or swoop over his head, scolding and screaming, demanding their share.

Hank Burroughs came down on the sand where Josh was stepping the mast of *Scorch*.

"Hey, Josh, lay a fact on me, willya?"

Since he'd discovered that Josh was attempting to go through the encyclopedia on his own free time, Hank had got into this habit of asking for a quick fact. In the beginning it had been sort of annoying and Josh had told him to go read his own facts, but after a while it developed into sort of a game.

"Anteaters don't have any teeth."

"How do they chew?"

"They don't. They snuffle and suck."

"We back to the A's?"

"Nope. I just happened to remember it. Thought it was something you better know."

"Well, I mean, you just got to me in time. Here I might've been with some important people and let slip my ignorance about no teeth in anteaters. Thanks a bunch. You gonna go out? Can I come? Be practically your last chance to enjoy my companionship—we're going to Nantucket end of the week."

"Okay."

Josh got his new red-and-white-striped Dacron sail and attached it to the mast, and they shoved off from the beach, feet in the cockpit, luffing for a few hundred feet.

"You're too close to the wind," Hank observed.

"Gee thanks. I'd never of guessed," Josh said, moving the tiller. "You just duck, because I'm gonna jibe."

The boom swung over them as they switched to starboard and headed into the bay.

"How far've ya got?" Hank asked. "I mean, in your old E.B.?"

"To the D's," Josh said shortly. He was still put out at the way they poked fun at him for his reading, but found it difficult to remain annoyed for long. "You want to hear about dinosaurs?"

"Not everything, not all at once. But you can give me the—"

"I know, the bare bones. Very funny."

Hank shrugged, and they leaned back as the sail filled and *Scorch* flew before a low following wave. "You really gonna go all the way through it?" he asked after a bit. "The *Encyclopædia Britannica*, I mean?"

39

"If you think it's such a squirrelly notion, why d'ya keep asking me about it?"

"I guess that's because why. I just can't figure a thing like that. Reading when you don't have to. You're something else, all right, Josh old buddy. Tell me something, do you remember all that junk—that information you read?"

Josh didn't reply right away. Actually, he'd already forgotten much of what he'd read. For instance, back there under B, he'd found thirty-three people named Brown and seven named Browne, and the only one he now recalled a thing about was John Brown, who raised up the slaves and was killed at Harpers Ferry, and the only reason he remembered him was that they'd studied about him in school.

There were times when he found the whole enterprise pretty dumb, times when he found it overwhelming, seeing how far he had to go, and times when he wished they didn't have an *Encyclopædia Britannica* at all. Of course in a house as full of books as theirs, there was bound to be some sort of encyclopedia, and it had just been his own tongue-wagging that had put him in the position of having to read from the A.B.C. Powers to zygote.

Just the same, thinking it over, he decided that wasn't so, and that he'd go on reading it even if nobody ever listened to anything he said, instead of just almost to nothing. Because it was something he'd decided on his own to do, and for some funny reason that was the kind of thing he had to go on with. At times he was tempted to quit, or to skip. And he had to admit he skimmed plenty. Differential equations, ordinary. Differential equations, partial. Differential geometry. Differential psychology. He'd given all that less than total attention. And looking ahead a little after Dinosaur, he saw he was about to run into Diophantine equations, which was sort of a downer, but if he moved right along pretty soon he'd get to a history of diving, and that ought to be pretty good.

In any case, he'd found out something about himself just getting from the A's to the D's, and that was that it was just about impossible to cheat on himself. He was prepared, if driven to it, to lie to his parents, or cheat on an exam—his parents being pretty hard to live up to sometimes, and his last year's teacher, Mr. Greene, being about as mean-tempered a guy as you could find (who wouldn't have been able to tell a live baby seal from a football). But he couldn't cheat on himself, no way. It was interesting. Besides, he hadn't set himself any time limit. He could take till he was ninety-four or even a hundred to finish up.

"There's some people moving into Senator Freebee's house," Hank said.

"I know. I saw their furniture."

"You call that stuff *furniture*? I betcha they turn out to be blacks, or white trash. My father's gonna go right through the ceiling when he gets back."

Josh didn't think a man who fell down his own front

steps and tossed his cookies on the lawn had a right to go through the ceiling about anything anybody else was or did, but you didn't say something like that to a friend. He supposed Hank was his friend, even if they didn't like each other all that much. Living at Lands End, he didn't know enough kids his age to be all that fussy about who was a friend.

He settled for, "Maybe they're just poor."

Fat Matt was probably right when he said the zoo paid lousy salaries. Wasn't that why Dr. Beldon had switched to pussycats and poodles? To Josh's way of thinking, to be a zoo veterinarian would be such a super job that he wouldn't care if they paid him at all. But Dr. Beldon must've thought different. Or his wife had. Anyway, he wasn't going to discuss the new vet's furniture with Hank, who was an all right guy in a few ways, but sneered at people he thought were beneath him, an idea he'd been taught by his gasbag of a father. Josh felt an upsurge of pride, of affection, for his own father, who didn't like humanity, he said, but did not consider himself to be *above* anybody.

"Coming about!" he yelled.

They scrambled to port and Hank said, "You could give a little more notice, like, you know."

Josh smiled to himself and said nothing. It was true —on the water he not only didn't want anyone else talking, he didn't want to talk himself. He wished he'd lived in the time when boys like him could run away to sea, starting out as horribly mistreated cabin boys and rising to be captains of their own square-rigged four-masters. Or, on the other hand, maybe hanged, like Billy Budd. He'd read *Billy Budd, Foretopman* twice. The best and saddest book he'd ever read in his life. Sometimes he thought he'd like to be like Billy Budd —honestly, all-the-way-through *good*. And lovable. They'd all loved Billy Budd, even if in the end they'd hanged him because of their dumb rules of the sea. Would it be worth being hanged to be loved and admired and *respected* the way Billy—who wasn't much older than Josh, come to that—had been? He sighed, and supposed not. He supposed he didn't really want to run away. He just thought about it sometimes, that was all.

"Why aren't you saying anything?" Hank asked irritably. "What're you doing, squinting out to sea like an old sea dog?"

Surprised that Hank had come anywhere close to what he'd actually been thinking, Josh said, "There's a squall coming. Look."

On the horizon a dark haze had appeared as suddenly as a dropped curtain, and already seabirds were dropping to the waves or heading shoreward. For a moment Josh's red-and-white sail shuddered as the wind changed, and then he came about without remembering to call out, nearly hitting Hank with the boom.

"Some sea dog," Hank muttered, when they were

on the opposite deck, leaning far out as *Scorch* skated over the bay, grown pewter-colored and choppy, toward home.

Dropping his sail just in time to keep from soaring over the beach into the palmettos, Josh saw his father walking down the dock toward them. *Candide* was rising and falling at her mooring, and the skiff, tied to a dock piling, was bucking at the lines.

"Could've dropped your sail sooner," said Mr. Redmond as he approached them. "Hello, Hank."

"Good afternoon, sir."

Like Josh's other friends, Hank held Mr. Redmond somewhat in awe and didn't warm to him. Now he waved and said, "See you," to Josh and was off as the first drops of rain began to spit at them. The wind from the sea was fresh and almost cool. It rustled in the palm fronds with a whistling sound, and set the feathery top branches of the Australian pines tossing. On the beach, shallow waves slapped with the rising tide, and the waters surged heavily around the pilings of the dock.

Josh flared his nostrils at all this with utter pleasure. All at once the rain was drenching and they ran for the house, where Mrs. Redmond was dashing from room to room hurling windows down.

"Get the kitchen door, will you, Josh?" she called. "And turn on the radio so we can get the weather report."

Josh went into the kitchen, secured the screen door

44

and the inside door, and turned on the radio. His glance fell on the bulletin board, where his notice still blocked out most of the other items.

I AM NOT GOING TO TALK
ANYMORE, SO NOBODY
TALK TO ME BECAUSE I
WON'T ANSWER.

He looked at it a bit grimly, removed the thumbtacks, stuck them back on the board, tore up his sign, and dropped it in the wastebasket. It wasn't the first dopey idea he'd had and it sure wouldn't be the last.

"Hey, Dad, Mom," he shouted, going down the hall toward the living room where his parents were sitting side by side on the sofa looking out the window. They loved to watch a storm. "Hey, did you know there's a new vet coming to be at the zoo? I saw their furniture being put in Tincture of Spain and it's sure—" His voice trailed off and he studied their faces. "Ah, for the luvva mud—"

He turned, having in mind to go up to his own room and watch the storm from there. Even if he talked to himself, the only person he'd interrupt would be himself, and he didn't mind being interrupted.

"Joshua," said his father.

He looked over his shoulder. "Yeah?"

"Come on in and help us keep an eye on this gale, will you?"

"Yeah, but how d'ya know I won't forget and

accidentally *say* something? I mean, I might *talk* or something, and then where would we be?"

"Knock it off," said Mr. Redmond. "Self-pity is a narcotic, Josh. It's habit-forming. You're too young to get started on the drug habit. Tell you what, we'll make a bargain. Every *third* time you enter a room, try to remember to come in as if—as if you were still bound by that oath you tacked to the board. Just every third time, come in without talking."

Josh thought it over. "You've got a deal," he said. Maybe, he thought. He supposed it was a trick he could try all right, but who could remember when was the third time he'd come into a room?

Sitting with his parents, eyes on the rolling, bunching, bellying waters over which the rain and wind rampaged, he was contentedly silent. He thought about the ocean, trackless and vast, where the whale swam, singing as the porpoises sang. What was in the whale's enormous brain? Hunted over all the seas of the world, the whales, like the cheetahs, were doomed to extinction. Josh thought that the whale, with his marvelous brain, might even have figured this out, and if he'd been a real fish might have sounded, gone to the depths, to outwait man and only surface again when he was gone. But the whale had to breathe air, and men with their machine guns could find him anywhere.

"When I grow up," he said, "I'm going to work at saving the endangered species. Whales and polar bears and tigers and like that." If there're any endangered species left to save, he thought, knowing strangely that his father was thinking the same thing and being good enough not to say it to him.

He sighed and wriggled in his chair while thoughts crowded in his head, waiting to be enworded. Enworded. Had he made that up? It was pretty good. He glanced at his parents, thinking to share it, but they were all caught up in the storm. For a while he watched them watching it. He realized that when they tried to teach him manners, consideration for other people's feelings, that sort of thing, they were thinking of his own good. In a way, he could see that somebody who talked all the time could be considered maybe rude. And could wind up a bore. Look at Fat Matt. Okay, his father and mother were thinking of his own good. The trouble was, he didn't want to do things for his own good. Anyway, not the "own" part of him they were concentrating on. He wanted to do things for—his wild spirit's good. And that was what nobody would understand. He guessed that was probably why he loved birds so much, and animals that weren't in cages. Birds and wild animals lived for their own spirits' sakes and for nothing else.

5

Unlike the parents of some other kids he knew, Josh's mother and father never quarreled, never set the air between them shaking with rage, or even, like Hank's folks, with what sometimes seemed plain hatred. When they were together, his parents seemed easy and fond of each other. Not soupy fond, like Clooney Powers' mother and father who, even at their age, were always holding hands or patting each other or even kissing in front of other people and Josh didn't see how Clooney put up with it, though on the other hand he didn't see what Clooney could do about it either. And with the exception mainly of trying to get him not to talk so much, his own mother and father didn't nag.

Like this afternoon, he thought now, watching the sea grape with its plate-large leaves writhe in the driving rain just outside the window, this afternoon when I came in like a B-52 and only just got the sail down in time to keep from crashing into the palmettos, all Dad said was, "Could've dropped your sail sooner." He didn't shout at me, or fuss because I hadn't got in earlier, or fume because I'd gone out at all, although I didn't know there was a squall coming any more than he did.

And his mother never hovered over him. He never got back from, say, a clamming or a shell-collecting expedition hours later than he said he'd be back, to find her in tears or on the horn to the cops, the way Mrs. Burroughs or Mrs. Powers would certainly be if Hank or Clooney was out somewhere with the dark and the tide coming in.

No, looked at from most angles, his parents were just about ideal. He looked at his ideal parents now and burst out, "*Why* don't you fuss and fume at me? That's what I don't understand. Like for Pete's sake, don't you care if I get home late or get caught in a squall? Don't you care what happens to me at all?"

The three of them were still in the living room, watching the storm rail on the waters. Down at the end of the dock an occasional wave was flung high and dashed along the wooden boards in a tumbling fall that sluiced and flattened and ran over the sides. Although it was only seven o'clock, it was quite dark, and his father had lit the lanterns out there on the farthest piles, one on each side of the dock. They were stationary, but seemed in the wind and the driving rain and the surrounding blackness to flicker and sway. The light from them flashed on the cresting and falling waves in gold, pitching streaks.

Mrs. Redmond seemed lost in contemplation of the scene and didn't reply, but after a moment Josh's father said, "I don't think I understand. What do you mean we don't care—or do we care—or whatever you said, about what happens to you?"

"I mean," said Josh, aware that he was whipping himself into a fury and quite unable to stop, "that nobody around here gives a—a darn if I get home or get eaten by a giant clam, that's what I mean."

Mrs. Redmond turned now and studied her son's face. "What a ridiculous thing to say, Josh. Why do you say it? You know it isn't so." She sounded tired, as if she'd said all this before, which, as it happened, she had.

But Josh persisted. "How do I know it isn't so? You don't care if I get home late. I got home about sixteen hours later the other day than I told you I'd be and when I got here you were reading a *book*."

"What should I have been doing? Calling the Coast Guard?"

"Hank Burroughs' mother would've called them, all right. She's always calling them."

"Would it please you if we did the same?"

"No," he snapped. "But you could've at least been —maybe out on the beach looking for me, couldn't you?"

50

"I didn't know which direction you'd taken; besides—"

"You didn't care which direction I'd taken!" By now his throat was aching because he wanted to cry but wouldn't, and he was shaking with rage at them, at himself, at everything. Gusts of fury like this seemed to come up in him as suddenly as summer squalls, and there was about as much he could do to prevent one as the other. Even as he was shouting things he wasn't altogether sure he believed, he was beginning to feel a little sick to his stomach, wishing, too late as usual, that he'd never got started.

He wasn't sure what had set him off this time. He never really knew. He'd been doing this sort of thing all his life. When he'd been much smaller, he'd had a habit of banging his head against a wall until he raised real bumps. He didn't do that anymore, but these explosions still took hold of him and he still couldn't predict when they were coming, or understand why they came.

His parents were paying attention to him now, all right. They'd forgotten about studying the storm. They had their eyes fixed on his face, and their expressions were alert and concerned. It still wasn't what he wanted, what he was looking for. He didn't know what he wanted or was looking for.

All at once he slumped in his chair, tired and indifferent. He heard his mother say that as a matter of fact she had gone out on the beach to look for him, several times, heard his father say that their not fussing and fuming, as he chose to put it, was a mark of their trust in him, their respect for his judgment. "If you weren't the sailor you are, I'd probably worry," he said. "But you know how to handle a boat, how to watch the weather. If you didn't, we wouldn't let you have a boat. But you're a born sailor."

"Yeah, I'll bet," said Josh in a low voice. He liked what his father was saying and hoped, by seeming not to believe the words, to hear some more along the same lines. About how well, maybe, he crewed on *Candide*. About how he hadn't panicked that time he and his father had been coming down from St. Pete and had run into a fog bank and had had to sail home for hours practically blind. Things like that.

But Mr. Redmond got up, saying he had work to do, and went off to his study. Josh looked after him bleakly.

"He told you the truth," said Mrs. Redmond. "And the fact is, you knew it. You're quite aware that we trust you with boats, but you ought to know better than to try tricks like that with your father."

"Tricks like what?"

"Josh, we aren't stupid. You wanted him to go on and on telling you what a fine sailor you are, and he'd already said it. Why do you always need more?"

Josh didn't know the answer to that, but he did think that if he needed more words his father could've stuck around and supplied a few. What would he waste? A couple of minutes? A few breaths of air?

"I'm going in to get dinner. Want to help me?"

He shook his head.

"All right. If you change your mind, come along. I could use some help now and then, you know."

He heard her leave but continued to lie half off his chair, regarding his big feet and listening to the rain dash against the windows. He was so full of anger at both of them that for a moment he was tempted to rush into the whirling windy dark and take his boat out and get drowned and that'd show them. But he didn't move for a long time, and then he fell asleep so that his mother had to wake him for dinner, which she did by leaning over to kiss him lightly on the top of his head.

"Nobody," she said, "but a boy could possibly sleep in such a ridiculous position."

Josh struggled to his feet, yawning, uncertain of the time or where he was. "Wassa matter?" he mumbled.

"Nothing. It's dinnertime, and we'd like the pleasure of your company. After you've washed."

He stumbled off to the downstairs bathroom to wash his hands and dash cold water on his face, which woke him sufficiently to recall that he'd fallen asleep in a rage but couldn't remember why. And this, too, was the way it always was. He'd work himself up till he felt like a bomb bursting in air, and then when it passed, he couldn't, without concentrating, remember what it had all been about.

He preferred not to concentrate that hard.

As they ate fish chowder and corn bread and salad,

one of Josh's favorite meals, Mr. Redmond said, "So there's somebody moving into that Fantasia Espagnole down the way?"

"It's the new zoo vet, his name is Arthur, Dr. Arthur, and they're driving here from Ohio, him and his family, but had their furniture sent before and Dr. Claven sent Fat Matt over to oversee getting it all in safely, but Hank Burroughs says the furniture is so tacky they're probably blacks or white trash and his father is going to go through the ceiling when he—"

"Joshua!"

"Huh? What, Dad?"

Mr. Redmond was breathing heavily. "Joshua, do *not* use the term white trash. Ever."

"I was only saying what Hank said."

"And he, undoubtedly, was parroting his jackass of a father. You are not to pick up their habits of speech, or their way of thinking. I won't have it."

"It's okay to say black?"

"Negroes themselves say black. I've never heard anyone describe himself as white trash and no one will be so described in our house."

"Well, I saw this furniture they've got myself, and it sure looks junky."

"That has nothing to do with using terms that demean yourself and other people. Don't use expressions for people that they wouldn't use themselves."

"Okay, okay," Josh said impatiently. Couldn't they

54

ever stop correcting him, even for a little while? He wondered, briefly, why it was that he got angry when they trusted him to the point where they could calmly read a book no matter where or how late he was, but also got angry when they cared so much about his manners that they couldn't pay attention to his point. He couldn't come up with an answer, but he sure got tired of being improved in the middle of a sentence. Did anybody but himself ever need so much correcting? Or was it that his parents needed more than most other people to be correcting somebody? His father had about thirty men working for him at the chandlery. Couldn't he get his kicks out of bossing them? His mother was in about eighty thousand volunteer organizations for improving people's condition, including she counseled delinquent children, so with all of them to work out on, why did she have to be counseling her own kid all the time, too?

"Well, I was only trying to tell you about who was coming into that house, that's all. Fat Matt counted their beds and he says—"

"While we're on the subject of what we do and don't call people," said Mrs. Redmond, "I do *not* think Fat Matt is a pleasant way in which to address an elderly man."

"Well, let me tell you," said Josh triumphantly, "that he calls *himself* that. All the time. So there. I mean, if I'm not supposed to use expressions for people that they wouldn't use themselves, then I *am* supposed to call them what they do call themselves. Right? And Fat Matt calls himself Fat Matt. He says, 'They ain't no flies on Fat Matt, no sirree, they ain't.' That's exactly what he says, or things like that. So what's the matter with me calling—"

"What's the matter with *my* calling," said his mother. "The possessive pronoun is used in cases where—"

Josh stood up.

"Sit down, Josh," said his father. "You haven't finished your meal."

"I haven't finished a sentence, either," said Josh, remaining on his feet. "People are all the time so busy telling me how I should say something that nobody listens to what I'm saying. Besides, you interrupt me. You're all the time telling me not to interrupt, so why's it okay if you do it?"

Mr. and Mrs. Redmond looked at each other and back to Josh.

"Right you are," said Mr. Redmond. "We've been interrupting you, and it's rude, and we apologize, Josh. Sit down, please."

Mrs. Redmond added, "I admit it, we've been a little too instructive this evening. Please do go on with what you were telling us."

Instructive, thought Josh. Boy. They're like a couple of traffic cops. "I forget what I was saying," he muttered.

"No," said his father. "You remember all right. You were telling us about the new veterinarian for the zoo who's moving into the old Freebee house."

Josh shrugged. "So. I've told you. He's the new vet and he's moving here. So?"

"Mealtimes are known to be the periods of greatest tension in American families," said Mrs. Redmond. "It's a shame, since it's one of the few times the family is together."

"Which may account for the tensions," said her husband.

"Well, it's bad for the digestion and bad for the spirit. I think we should make a resolution that in the future we put aside our differences and our worries when we come to the table, and just concentrate on being pleasant to one another. Shall we put it to a vote?"

Mr. Redmond laughed. "Sounds to me like one of your committee meetings. But okay, I second the motion. I assume you've made a motion?"

She nodded, smiling, and they turned to Josh.

"All those in favor?" said Mrs. Redmond.

Wow, thought Josh. Oh boy. He looked about him, as if the brother he always wished he had would somehow materialize because of his terrible need. It wasn't fair to leave one kid alone with a pair of parents like this. It was just downright not fair.

"We're waiting for you to cast your ballot, Joshua."

"Mine's secret," he mumbled.

"Oh come on, now, Josh," said Mr. Redmond. "We're trying to make amends."

Josh took a deep breath, exhaled, and said, "I vote aye."

"The ayes have it," said Mr. Redmond. "Good. Well, what shall we talk about?"

Mrs. Redmond said, patting Josh's hand, "What are you up to in the encyclopedia?"

"Diphtheria."

"Excellent. Tell us about it," Mr. Redmond directed.

That night Josh lay in bed listening to the storm, thinking stormy thoughts. It was a bit too early in the season for hurricanes, but he wished some hurricane that didn't know about seasons would come down the coast and carry everything out to sea. The trouble was that even in hurricanes, houses on the bay side were pretty safe. It was the intrepid (reckless, his father said) people who built on the Gulf side who were forever trying to collect insurance because part or all of their houses were underwater or blown down or blown away.

Actually, long ago in a tropical storm that still lived in legend, this house that his grandfather built had been flooded up to the window ledges so that water and sand had poured in all over the ground floor, and the dock had been destroyed by huge seas that came up everywhere and washed clean over the island. In the family album there were pictures of the house and dock

58

as things had been then, the house much smaller, the dock bigger. After the waters had receded, leaving sea wrack and rubbish everywhere, in the house and all around it, his grandfather and father had set to work and rebuilt, with the help of a carpenter now, like his grandfather, a long time dead.

They'd done some pretty good things, like putting in all new windows that had louvers so you could leave them open in all but the heaviest weather. They'd put on a new roof, aluminum, and put on a whole new addition to the house, making the living room bigger and giving his father a study. They'd put in electricity and running water. Josh sort of regretted this. He thought it would be far nicer to live by the light of oil lamps, and take a bath once a week in a big old copper tub in the kitchen, which was how his father used to do when he was a kid. In some of the pictures in the album there were (accidentally, he was sure) a couple of views of the old outhouse. It had a wooden hand on it that people would put up when they were in the privy to warn other people to stay away.

Josh, when he'd seen this, had said, "Hey, what a gas," and his mother had thought he was making a pun and had said it was in bad taste.

But since that time, long before Josh's birth, there'd never been such heavy waters on the bay side again, though the dock after all the years was once more being undermined by the constant movement of tide. Mr.

Redmond kept saying he was going to do something about it, but he didn't.

Josh got out of bed and went to the window seat; he sat with his chin on his knees, looking out into the dark at the flashing red lights of channel markers. Rain drummed on the dock and on the aluminum roof with a deafening sound. Waves thudded on the beach. He hoped he'd pulled *Scorch* far enough up on the sand.

Had he?

He'd pulled her up as far as he usually did, but was that going to be far enough tonight, in this storm that seemed to him to be increasing in spite of the weather report saying it would all be blown out to sea by morning?

Getting a flashlight, he crept out of his room, along the hall, and downstairs through the kitchen. He had no idea of the time, but everything was in darkness except for the lights at the end of the dock. So his parents were asleep, which was a relief. Letting himself out the kitchen door, he ran over the sand and found that *Scorch* and the canoe were, after all, safely far from the tide.

A big heron that had been roosting on the back porch took alarm at his approach and flapped into the dark with a hoarse-sounding *craack-craack*. Josh listened, grinning. They always sounded so enraged if you disturbed them at night, and never learned that there wasn't any need, that they could just go on sleeping peacefully for all he was going to bother them.

60

The warm gusty wind whipped his pajama shorts, winding them wetly around his legs, and he was soaked in just this brief time. But it was great, just great. He stood with his arms stretched out, head up, mouth open to catch the driving raindrops. Out on Catfish Island, uninhabited except by birds and snakes and raccoons, he thought he heard the owl shriek, but through the moaning, singing sound of the wind he couldn't be sure.

After a few minutes, wet as if he'd been swimming, and entirely happy, he went back into the house, stripped off his soaking pajamas, dried himself, and went to bed, this time to sleep.

6

In the morning only a freshness in the placid air recalled the wind and the rain that had passed over the
island. The waters of the bay were blue and scarcely
rippled. From his window seat, Josh looked out at a
world filled with birds. Skimmers and sea gulls and
terns flashed in flocks over the waves. Out on a sandbar
exposed by the tide, grave brown pelicans were taking
their ease, and on Catfish Island white egrets moved
along the shore or roosted in the branches of fallen
trees. On dock pilings and channel markers dark cormorants stood watch, and just below Josh's window, on
the jetty, a little green heron sat with neck tucked so
close into his body that he looked like a chicken.

"Josh? Joshua, are you up?"

"Yup."

"What are you doing?"

"Looking at birds. Mom, look out the kitchen window, you can see a kingfisher. He's sitting right next to a sea gull at the end of the jetty. They've got their eye on something, all right."

"Dear, come down for breakfast, will you? Your father's already at the table."

"Right there."

For some reason he never was really hungry in the morning, but for some other reason his parents liked to have all three of them together at breakfast and even wanted them all to eat the same things. It was a matter of coordinating things, his father said. His father said a family was like a corporation, and a corporation can't run smoothly unless everyone takes his share of the work and the responsibility.

Josh couldn't see why a corporation would run smoothly because he ate eggs, which he hated. He didn't even see why a corporation had to run smoothly, especially if it wasn't a corporation at all but a family. He wished he could nerve himself to say something like this to his father. Not like arguing, just discussing. Why was it so hard to discuss things with his parents? He could tell them facts, when they felt like listening, and he could listen while they told him facts—if he felt like listening. But they never just all three of them talked about something.

"Good morning, Joshua," said his father, laying aside the newspaper he'd been looking at.

"Morning." His father looked at him, waiting, so Josh added, "Sir."

Well, it was all very difficult. For instance, like now. He simply did not feel, at the moment, like calling his father Dad, which he usually did. He'd never called him Pop, which was what Hank called his old man, and he had never, even in his mind, thought of his father as his old man. He could hardly start with Father after years of Dad. What it came to was just now he'd have preferred not to call his father anything except "you." But his parents would never permit him just to say yes or no or good morning to anyone. He had to add something, like the person's name, or Mom or Dad. Or *sir*. He figured maybe he was the only kid in his class who ever called his father sir. That was okay for teachers and the doctor and people like that. But your own father?

Josh sat down, his humor already ruined with the day hardly started, and his mother came in with eggs. A plate of bacon and eggs for each of them. Two eggs for his father, one each for Josh and herself. Josh stared at his, lying there, the center part bulbous and yellow, the white part flat and not hard enough. It was flanked by two pieces of bacon. The bacon was crisp and he wouldn't mind eating it. But that egg.

"Look, Mom—" he began.

"Now, dear," she said, smiling, going back to the kitchen for toast and returning to her seat. "Now, Josh. Don't start at me about eggs. Twice a week is not too often to ask you to eat one little egg."

64

Josh figured twice a year was too often. Twice in a lifetime was too often to ask someone to eat eggs who didn't like eggs.

"I don't like eggs. Besides, my teacher Mr. Greene said eggs have cholesterol in them and cholesterol fattens up the blood vessels and that is *not* good for a person. In fact, if we want to be very healthy, we should all stop eating eggs. I mean, do you want us to have fat blood vessels?"

"The only time you ever quote Mr. Greene with approval," said Mr. Redmond, putting a fork in his yolks so that they ran over the whites, "is when he's said something that backs up some prejudice of your own."

Josh, looking away from his father's plate, said, "That about cholesterol isn't prejudice. It's a scientific fact and I don't see how you don't know about it. I mean, you're such a smart man, and all," he said with conviction. His father was, really, one of the smartest men anywhere. "How come you don't know about cholesterol?"

"I do know about it. I know that eggs eaten to excess are not good for a person. But then, anything eaten to excess, anything done to excess, is harmful. That does not mean we're required to abjure altogether the eating of eggs."

Josh was finding the repetition of the word egg too much for his stomach. "Mom," he said weakly, "I don't feel good. Honest."

65

"Then go back to bed, dear. I'll take your temperature and if you have a fever I'll call the doctor."

"I don't have a fever!" Josh said loudly. "I only just don't want to eat an egg. It's making me sick, looking at it. Look," he said, lowering his voice with an effort. "Can't I just eat the toast and bacon and have a cup of coffee?"

"A cup of coffee. You won't eat an egg, which is good for you and I don't care what Mr. Greene says, and you're asking for a cup of coffee?"

The thought of a nice strong drink of coffee laced with sugar and milk was so appealing to Josh that he could almost taste it. Sometimes, when he was alone in the afternoon, he'd make himself a mug of it and go out on the dock and sit in an old redwood chair his grandfather had made and sip peacefully, tossing scraps of bread to the sea gulls and dreaming up things to do when he was old enough to start doing something.

Save the endangered species, or maybe train porpoises and learn to talk with them. Or design boats, or go into business with Clooney Powers. He and Clooney thought that in addition to the Bait and Tackle Shop Mr. Powers ran, they'd add a marina, and maybe a small ships chandlery. Not a big one, like his own father's, because that was too much work. Just a little one, for small boats. Or maybe he'd just filch from other people's crab pots (always rebaiting them, of course, following a course of honorable thievery) and be dishonest and independent at the same time. In any case, when he grew up, he didn't figure on working very hard. What did a guy need out of life, except a shack to live in, a canoe, a skiff with a ten-horsepower motor, and a good sailboat? He ought to be able to manage that without killing himself working.

He'd sit out there on the dock with his coffee and his thoughts, and somehow coffee was part of the whole satisfying time.

And he thought that if they'd let him have coffee with his breakfast it would start every day better, and maybe even help him choke the damned egg down twice a week. Why did they have to have so many rules? And anyway, if they had to have them, did they have to stick to them all the time? He thought that when he grew up he'd have rules, too. A whole raft of rules, and he'd break them whenever he wanted to.

By now his parents had cleaned their plates and were discussing the storm and how it had, after all, blown out to sea just as the weatherman had predicted, which was a surprise. Not that the storm had gone, but that the weatherman had predicted it would.

"Astonishing," his father was saying, "how often these fellows with all their instruments contrive to be wrong in their forecasts, when my father could predict accurately ninety per cent of the time with nothing but his weatherwise instinct to go by. Joshua, do you propose to sit in front of that egg all day? Your mother and I are finished, and I have to leave for work."

So leave, thought Josh. He looked up, sighed, picked

up his fork, put it down again, and said, "Okay. I guess I sit here all day. I can't eat it."

"Oh, for heaven's sake," said Mrs. Redmond. "I can't stand this any longer. Go and throw it to the sea gulls."

"Sure thing." Josh grabbed the two pieces of bacon and the toast in his right hand, the plate with the egg on it in his left.

"Joshua!"

"Yeah? I mean—what is it? Dad."

"Either you eat everything on your plate or nothing. Throw it all out for the gulls."

"But I—"

"All of it, or eat your egg."

"Oh, for crud's sake," Josh yelled. He stamped out the kitchen door and down the dock, where he threw eggs, bacon, and toast to the gulls, who appeared whirling over his head as soon as he stepped outside. They swooped and shrieked, catching the scraps on the wing. Josh was tempted to throw the plate too, but he was already in enough hot water without bringing it to boiling.

He dawdled, hoping that his father would have found he was late and had to leave without hanging around for another session of character improvement.

At about the middle of the dock, in very shallow water, was the cement block structure that his grandfather had built to encourage stone crabs to breed. There never were as many crabs now as there'd been in his grandfather's day, or even his father's day. These times you didn't apparently find anything in the waters around here in the sort of abundance there'd been before all the building and pollution got going.

Just the same—he peered over—just the same, the cement blocks and the scraps of food that the Redmonds dropped down there attracted enough crabs so that about once a month they could feast on stone crab claws. He and his father would put on bathing trunks and get down there, picking up each crab in turn and carefully removing just one claw, which would grow back in time. Some people, mostly tourists, when they went after stone crabs would just yank off both claws and toss the body back, which meant the crab would die, because it needed one claw to catch food with. But then some people, his father said, were natural savages and slobs. He never went so far as to say that natural savages and slobs were mostly tourists. He did not, he said, characterize people by religion, race, or region. But somehow the things that his father most disapproved of, like building motels and condominiums or living in them, were done by people from out of state.

There were several crabs down there now, nestled in the hollow centers of the cement blocks, almost camouflaged by a covering of green algae and seaweed. Josh lay down on the wooden planks, already warm though it was still early morning, and let his arms hang over the edge. The water beneath the dock, constantly moving, was gradually eroding the pilings. One day, unless they got it fixed, the whole dock was going to drop into the bay. They never got around to getting it fixed, and it seemed sturdy enough to Josh. He hoped it was. It was one of the best things to do, lie out here and look through the planks at the green and shadowy water, at the flowerlike sea anemones waving their thin tentacles, at the crabs stirring lazily in their cement cells.

He figured there were enough crabs so that he and his father could gather some claws any day now. If any day now they felt like doing something together again. These times came when he and his father had their vibes so wrong they could hardly be in a room together without crackling. And to Josh it seemed that his mother was just about always on his father's side. Some kids he knew had their mothers so much on their side that they couldn't stand it. Clooney Powers, for instance. He said his mother was always sticking up for him and his brothers and his sister, even when they didn't want to be stuck up for. She was all the time having fights with Mr. Powers because she said he was too hard on them. Clooney said it was like the Civil War all over again, his mother and father always battling and yelling at each other (when they weren't kissing and cooing) and mostly over whether one of the kids was going to get, or get to do, something or other. Clooney said that usually by the time the fighting stopped and they were smooching again he didn't want whatever it was anymore. All he wanted was some peace.

Well, Josh couldn't picture his father and mother slugging it out over anything, certainly not over *his* wants and wishes. What his father said went, period. He watched a pelican skim low over the water, wingtips barely clearing the waves. The pelican looked, from this angle, like a bow, and Josh never tired of watching them, the wonderful skillful fliers, soar with their feathered wingtips keeping just that fraction of an inch clearance.

He rolled to his back, crossing one leg over the other knee, and squinted at the sky. What to do today? Not a ripple of wind, so it was pointless to take *Scorch* out. He could fish, except he didn't feel like fishing. He could go round up Hank and see if he had anything in mind, except he was probably packing for Nantucket where he and the rest of the Burroughs family went every summer. Clooney, of course, would have been up long ago, out on the boat catching bait shrimp, and now he'd be at the shop working. Clooney was hardly ever free to do anything until late afternoon.

Josh got lazily to his feet, hearing his father's car go out of the turnaround.

A few yards away, on the jetty, the little blue heron stepped cautiously along on his string-thin legs, finding things to eat. Overhead a herring gull flew past with a needlefish in his beak. As Josh watched, the silvery fish slipped from the gull's beak, was caught by another, a laughing gull this time, who was assailed on all sides by other gulls until it looked like a football scrimmage with so much tackling and fumbling and passing that Josh lost track of who had the ball. It was the darndest thing about sea gulls, how they seemed to materialize from nowhere the second there was any food to be had.

Sometimes, watching birds, you got the feeling that they did nothing with their lives except search, search, search for food, and fight over it when the search turned anything up. And yet, afternoons out on the sandbars, on the channel markers, on the jetty, at the end of this dock, there they'd be—gulls, terns, cormorants, egrets, herons, pelicans—birds in the thousands, sitting peacefully. As if, like Josh himself, they had no idea of what to do. Except that the birds, with nothing to do, just did nothing, whereas Josh—or practically any person, he supposed—would always have to try to work up some activity or other. And even if you didn't *do* anything, you'd have to think. He wondered if birds thought about anything, had dreams, ever schemed. You got the impression from a raccoon, say, that he was always cooking up some plot. Josh never doubted for a second that a raccoon was thinking away as hard as he could all the time. Dogs, too. Maybe cats—like the jaguars and cheetahs at the zoo. They seemed to be brooding, turning over sad or hostile thoughts.

But birds? They, he thought, just flew, and looked

for food, and nested and rested and sang or croaked and —just were. He supposed that was why he liked them so much. They just were.

He found his mother in the kitchen, clearing up. She turned when he came in, with the slight sort of smile she got when he and his father had had a ruckus and she hoped they'd just forget about it and press on anew.

"There's some toast and bacon in the oven for you," she said.

"No thanks, Mom." She was, come to think of it, pretty often on his side.

"Oh, Josh. Don't sulk."

"I'm not sulking. It's—well, you know. I kind of made a bargain. All or nothing at all. I just like to keep bargains."

"I see." She sighed. "I think one of the difficulties with you and your father is that you're so much alike. Well, you needn't look as if I'd assailed your character—"

"That wasn't how I was looking. I was looking surprised."

"Just the same—both of you have a kind of honorable rigidity about life. It's admirable, but doesn't, I think, make for complete happiness."

"I don't know what that means. Honorable rigidity."

"Oh, I think you do."

"No, honest." He looked at her attentively, waiting for some more talk about his character.

"It means that you're both upright and stubborn.

Very little *give* to either of you. Well, I'm about finished here. I have a board meeting at the Mental Health Center this morning. What are you going to do?"

"Dunno."

She looked at him so closely that Josh turned his eyes away uneasily.

"Josh, are you happy?" she asked abruptly.

"What about?"

"Not *about* anything. Are you a happy person?"

"Why shouldn't I be?"

"Will you stop answering a question with another question?"

"Well, I have to answer something, and it seems to me—" He broke off.

"Yes? It seems to you what?"

"Well, it seems to me a dumb sort of question, that's all. I'm sorry, Mom. I just don't see how to answer a question am I happy. If I say I am, so what? And if I say I'm not, so what too? I mean, what would you do about it? Send me to a head doctor like you do your delinquent yo-yos?"

"Josh, please don't call those disturbed, unhappy children yo-yos. It's unkind. Not like you."

Well, it is like me, thought Josh, who knew he was frequently unkind in his thoughts, though not so often out loud. But his mother didn't know what he was like, any more than she knew if he was happy or unhappy. Come to that, he didn't know himself and didn't see why she had to ask him such a tomfool question. If that was the kind of thing they asked what they called "wayward youths," down at the mental health center, it was no wonder most of them went right on being delinquent.

Tell us, son, are you happy? If you aren't, explain why, in fifteen words or less.

Huh.

"I gotta go, Mom," he said.

"Where? You said you didn't know what you were going to do."

"I just thought of something."

"Josh, I'm trying to help you get to the root of your trouble, don't you see?"

"I don't have a trouble," he said loudly. "Except maybe there isn't any wind today, I don't have *a* trouble."

"You just won't be helped, will you?" she said in a sad tone.

"Mom, can I go now, please?"

"Of course you may. Go along."

"Well, look—I'm sorry if you want to help me and all. I mean, I'm sorry I don't need to be helped if you want to—" He stopped, shrugged. "I don't know what I mean."

"No. Well, I have to get ready. I'm sorry, Josh, that we don't have better communication, the three of us."

Josh, out on his bike, thought how earlier in the

morning he'd wished that he and his parents could just talk, but he hadn't meant talk like this, about him and his happiness. He'd meant just the three of them sitting around yakking about things, even discussing things, but things about the world, about bats or birds or Buddha or—

He pedaled along, thinking of answers he could've given his mother. Like—I'd be happy if you'd had two sons, or three. I'd be happy if I weren't an only child. Only he couldn't say something like that to his parents. To begin with, maybe it would hurt them. He didn't want to hurt them. To go on with it—pretty unthinkable but not altogether impossible—then maybe they'd have another kid. He couldn't stand that, no way.

Besides, maybe in some ways he was better off like this. Maybe—

He slowed down in front of Tincture of Spain. The cast-iron gates were open, and in the driveway was a Volkswagen camper that made Josh whistle. Looks like a piece of salvage, he said to himself. Looks like some hulk winched out of a mangrove swamp after years of being nibbled at by underwater monsters. Looks like it wouldn't hold together long enough to back out of the drive. Wow.

Music burst through the downstairs windows; it sounded as if about fifty kids were bawling in there. A man's voice was telling everybody to shut up for Pete's sake he was trying to talk on the phone, and now, from around the side of the house, came a skinny old guy with a beret who walked up to Josh and said, "You there, young fellow, get to work now, get to work, the rest of them are coming in and coming in and coming in and you can do it too but not upside down that way if you see what I mean—there're all these people coming in and coming in and I want to know who are they—"

7

As he talked, the old man kept jabbing gently at Josh's shoulder with his finger.

Josh, stupefied and a little alarmed, backed off. But despite the jabbing finger and the strange words, the old man had such a cheery expression that Josh said, "How do you do, sir. Are you the new family moving in?"

"Well, I wouldn't say that. But I will say this." The old man stopped and Josh waited, but apparently that was the end of the thought. It was a moment before the old man resumed.

"Who are they?" he demanded, looking over Josh's shoulder. "That big one, there, coming here, who are they?"

Josh glanced back. There was no one there. "Uh— ah—good-bye, sir. I gotta go. Good-bye."

"Good-bye, is it? Good-bye. Fair enough, fair enough. Good-bye. Just a second—who's leaving, you or me?"

In spite of himself, Josh smiled, and at that the old man began to laugh heartily. "Yes, that's a good one, isn't it? That's good, yes indeed. We can laugh about that, all right. Tell you the truth, I think you'll do. Just have to try hard and you'll do it even before the others. They're not halfway, you know."

"Hey, Granddad, where are you—oh, there you are. Boy, I thought you'd got away from us."

A boy came bounding out of the house. He was perhaps Josh's age or a little older, but smaller, slenderer than Josh, who was a burly, curly-haired, muscular type like his own father.

The boy stopped when he saw the old man. "Granddad. I asked you to stay in the house, remember?"

"House, house? What house?"

"It's a new one, Granddad. We've moved, and we're living in this new house, this one right here."

"Is that a fact?"

"Fact."

Again the old man laughed with apparently genuine amusement. "An old new house. That's a good one, that is. Yes sir. Who're all these people going around and around us?"

"Just some fellows doing their job. Nobody to worry about."

"Oh, that's it, is it?"

"Yup. That's it. Why don't you go in the house now, Granddad, right up those steps. See if you can find Maureen."

Walking steadily, the old man went up the broad steps and disappeared into the house, still talking.

"He's my grandfather," the boy said, a bit combatively, to Josh. "He's got arteriosclerosis."

"Oh."

"Well, he isn't anyone to be afraid of. He's a nice old boy, and he used to be a great guy, really a great guy."

"Did I say something?"

"You looked something."

"No, I didn't. I was only talking with him. You gotta admit he's surprising, right off the bat that way."

"You were laughing."

"Oh, for cripes sake." Josh thought of leaving, but was too curious. "He said something funny, so I smiled, so what's wrong with that?"

The other boy relaxed. "Yeah. He does say some pretty funny things sometimes."

"Does he see people who aren't there?"

"All the time. But if you just tell him it's some people working, he isn't frightened. He's my dad's father, and Dad says he's always believed in the work ethic. I mean, Granddad's believed in it. But my father does, too. Boy, does he ever. We're lucky to see him fifteen minutes out of a week."

"Your father's the new zoo veterinarian?"

"He sure is," said the boy proudly.

"What's the work ethic?"

"People just working, instead of goofing off. Grand-dad used to be a carpenter, and until he got arterio-sclerosis, he worked ten, twelve hours a day every day of his life, practically. He still thinks work is the magic word. Not money. Work."

"What's arteriosclerosis?"

"Hardening of the arteries. It's affected his brain."

Josh recalled, vaguely, arteriosclerosis from the en-cyclopedia, but it was one of the subjects he hadn't troubled to absorb any information about.

"Are there arteries in the brain?"

"There are arteries everywhere in the body. Boy."

Again Josh made a move to leave, again changed his mind. "My name's Joshua Redmond."

"Ted Arthur."

They measured each other in tentative acceptance, and then, since there seemed to be nothing else to do, Josh said he'd be getting along.

"You can come in, if you want to," said Ted Arthur. "Place is a mess, of course, but it'll never change any. Every place we've lived in is a mess. It's on account of the animals."

"The animals?"

"We keep sort of getting animals dumped on us, my father being a vet. Back in Ohio we returned a couple of lion cubs to the zoo just the day before the moving men came. Cobina and Serena, we called them. Grand-dad used to go around saying Cobina and Serena live mainly on farina. He said it all the time. They tore up whatever we had left that was still in one piece, so now we don't have anything in one piece."

"You had lion cubs living with you? In your house?" Josh's eyes widened.

"Lion cubs, peccaries, aardvarks—you name it, we've housed it." Ted Arthur sounded offhand, but Josh didn't for a minute think he was. Briefly but keenly, he felt a thrust of envy. He, who had never even had a dog. But the concept of two lion cubs, or some aardvarks (he did recall them clearly, being the first interesting subject in the encyclopedia; a species of anteater, they were) or peccaries, but especially lion cubs, was too overwhelming to admit of prolonged envy. There was something more important here.

"I suppose," he said, trying to be casual, "you'll go on having them—animals, I mean—dumped on you here?"

"I should think so," Ted said with relish. "I mean, be-fore, when Dad worked at the university, we just got into the whole thing—taking baby animals, kind of by mistake, when my mother—" He paused, continued in a strained tone, "when my mother offered, at a bridge party, for Pete's sake, to take home a baby aardvark. Her partner was the zoo director's wife, and she'd been saying how she already had so many animals at

82

home she hardly had time to cook for her family. So, we got this aardvark. He used to follow us around like a puppy. Andy, we called him. And after that—well, *my* mother got so she hardly had time to cook for us. She was crazy about animals, all right."

Was? thought Josh.

"My mother," said Ted Arthur, with an air of wanting to get something said and finished with, "is dead. She died last year." He looked from side to side, met Josh's eyes glancingly, and stared at the ground. "That's why Dad took this job. He wanted to get away from—from there. We didn't especially want to come—I mean, the rest of us. Not," he added, "that that's anything against around here. I mean, we just had our friends and all—" He stopped again. "You wanna come in? I have stuff to do. Dad's going right over to the zoo and cripes knows when he'll ever get back."

Josh parked his bike against the iron gate and followed this boy, who seemed to be no slouch of a talker himself, into Senator Freebee's old house. He had been in Tincture of Spain just once before, on the day they cut old Freebee down, and it had all been a madhouse of people running around, so Chief Horton hadn't noticed him and Hank sneaking in until they'd already got to the living room. Hank had been sorry they weren't in time to see the body cut down from the rafter. But Josh, who'd been frightened and sort of sick to his stomach and had only gone along because Hank dared him to, thought it was horrible enough to see the ambulance men go by with Senator Freebee's body on a stretcher, all covered with a sheet and looking spooky as hell. That was when Chief Horton spied them and said, "Hey, you two—bug off. Whatcha think you're doin' here? Creeps," he'd said to one of his men, "that's what kids are these days. Creeps. Gettin' their jollies out of a thing like this."

Face flaming, Josh had shot out of the house and home, not waiting for Hank. Just the same, he'd had a chance to see the living room as it had been in the Senator's day—all rugs and books and pictures and polished furniture. Today the huge room looked practically empty. A couple of battered overstuffed chairs, some canvas chairs, that big old sofa he'd seen going in the other day, the table with tarnished fake brass legs, and a few straight-backed wooden chairs were dumped around. There were packing cartons, looking, as Fat Matt had said, trimmer than anything else in sight. There was an old crib against the fireplace wall.

"Ted, please help me get this stuff sorted out, will you?"

A thin girl a couple of years older than Ted but looking, in a girlish way, like him—same dark hair and blue eyes—came into the living room, her arms full of sheets and towels.

"Those oafs put all the bedroom stuff in the kitchen, so I guess the kitchen stuff is in one of the bedrooms, or in here. Hi," she said to Josh. "You from around here?"

"Yes, I—"

"It's so *hot*. I never knew a place could *be* so hot. It's horrible."

"I know," said Josh, feeling at fault but not knowing what to do about it. "I'm sorry."

"Oh, I'm not blaming you," she said, sounding as if she were.

"There ought to be—I should think there'd be air conditioning." He couldn't imagine that Senator Freebee would have gone without air conditioning. Most people around here had it. Not his house. But then, he and his parents liked the heat. It was only June now and not nearly as hot as it was going to get, but no need to go into that with them.

"The air conditioning doesn't work," said Ted. "We tried it. The whole joint is sort of crumbly, come to that."

"That's because it's been empty so long," Josh said. He wasn't going to mention Senator Freebee, on the chance that maybe they hadn't heard about him. He wouldn't, himself, want to live somewhere a guy had hanged himself. He glanced quickly up at the high center rafter. "On the Gulf here," he went on, "you gotta keep a house up or the ocean and the sea wind begin to move in on you and—"

He stopped as a man, who had to be Dr. Arthur,

came racing down the stairs two steps at a time. "My god, this place is an ark, a six-bedroom barracks. What could they have been thinking of, to rent a place like this to a family like ours for what's practically no rent at all? Something's screwy. Maybe they've made a mistake. I'd better see Dr. Claven before we unpack. Hullo, there," he said to Josh, and turned to Ted. "Pop's having the time of his life, going from room to room like driving pigs down a road in Connemara. You from around here?" he asked Josh.

"Yes sir. I—"

"Then maybe you'll know where the zoo's at?"

"Sure, I—"

"Mind showing me? I'm the new vet, but I've never even seen the place and I'd like to get over there. Maybe you can just tell me where it is."

"Sure, it's—"

Old Mr. Arthur came sailing down the banister and landed with a thud on his back.

"Oh, my God," said Dr. Arthur, as they all rushed to his father's side. "You okay, Pop? You hurt yourself? Can you sit up?"

Mr. Arthur sat up, rubbing the back of his head. "What's happening around here?" he asked severely. "Who did that?"

"You did it, Granddad," Ted Arthur said, relief in his voice. "You did it your own darnfool self. Now, cut it out, hear? You can't go sliding down the banisters, and that's that." He looked at his father. "Never thought of that, did we? We didn't have any stairs in our other house," he said to Josh. He looked up toward the second floor. "We'll have to put up gates. One at the top and one at the bottom. Otherwise he'll break his neck."

"That's right, that's right," said the old man. "You try hard enough and with both of us on the same side and nobody over there we'll come out even, whether it makes any difference or not." He struggled to his feet, brushing aside Ted's and Dr. Arthur's attempts to help. "Leave this to me, sir. Just leave this to me—I'll take care of them—"

"Watch him, will you?" Dr. Arthur said to Ted and Maureen. "I'll stop at a hardware store and get a couple of those folding gates they use for kids, but you'll have to keep an eye on him in the meantime."

"I also have to unpack and try to arrange the furniture and get to a market and cook dinner," said Maureen. "I'm not whining, you understand. I'm not even complaining. I'm only pointing out that—"

"Well, the boys here will help you, won't they?" said Dr. Arthur, and sped out the door without waiting for directions to the zoo.

"When you see me, that's how you'll know I'm back," said old Mr. Arthur, starting after his son.

Ted grabbed him by the arm, led him to one of the chairs, and turned it to face the sliding doors that led out to a flagstone terrace. "Not now, Granddad. That's some other time you were going."

"Is that a fact?"

"Fact. You sit here and look out at the birds. There're some sea gulls or something, down there on the beach."

"Ibises," said Josh. "And skimmers, and willets. Sandpipers. Sea gulls, too, of course." He wondered how anyone wouldn't know the difference, then recalled that probably in Ohio there weren't any sea gulls or ibises or willets or so forth.

"Yeah. Well, sit here and look at the ibises, etc., Granddad. Just stay put, okay?"

"Well, if you say so, if that's what you say—"

"That's what I say." Ted turned to his sister. "What'd you want me to do, Maureen?"

Maureen sank into an armchair, still holding the linen in her arms, and shook her head. "I don't know. I can't think. It's all—all—" Tears filled her eyes, and she leaned awkwardly around the bundle in her arms, trying to wipe them away with the back of her hand.

"Now, don't come unstuck," Ted said, alarm in his voice. "We've done just fine so far, let's not come unglued now. Please, Maureen."

"Oh, I'll be all right. It's just that—" She stopped, leaned her head back and closed her eyes. "Guess I'm just tired. And so hot."

"Here, I'll take this stuff," Ted said, grabbing the linen and piling it on one of the packing cartons.

"Maybe there's no point in unpacking anyway. Maybe Dad's right and this isn't the house we're supposed to be in. It's too big and fancy. In a grungey sort of way."

"It's the right house," said Josh.

They fixed their eyes on him.

"I know because I was talking to Fat Matt, he's one of the park guards; and he was guarding this place yesterday—"

"Guarding it?" Maureen snorted. "Against what?"

"So no one would—I don't know. So your furniture would get in safe or something. Dr. Claven sent him to oversee things, and it was your things, because he said your name, so this is the right house."

Ted laughed. "I wonder what he said when he saw what he had to oversee."

"Well—" He could hardly repeat Fat Matt's words. Or tell them that Fat Matt had figured, from counting one double bed, five twin beds, and a crib, that the Arthur family would arrive with a truckload of kids to go with the battered furniture. There was a crib, but no sign of a baby. If there were other children, where were they?

"Are Kev and Nora still asleep, Ted?"

"Last I saw they were. That was pretty nice. Of the moving men, I mean. They put up the beds for us."

"I expect Fat Matt made them," said Josh.

"Made the beds?" said Ted with a hoot. "Maureen did."

"Made the moving men put them up."

"What an awful thing to call anybody," said Maureen. "Fat Matt."

"He calls himself that. I think even his wife says Fatmatt, like it was one word, you know. I never heard anyone call him just Matt, come to think of it. Who're Kev and Nora?"

"Our brother and sister," said Ted. "Kevin's seven, and okay. Nora's four, and the biggest pain in the neck who ever lived."

"Oh Ted, stop," said Maureen. "She's a little girl and she's lonely—" Tears welled in her eyes again, and she walked away.

Josh and Ted looked at each other, and then Ted said, "Well, I gotta get to work. I mean, if this is really home sweet home, we'd better try to pull it together somehow. How're you doin', Granddad?" he called across the big room, his voice seeming to echo.

"Fine, fine," said the old man. "They're out there again, you know. Going around and around and around and ar—"

"Just doing their job, Granddad. They have to finish up, you know."

"Oh, of course, that's right, that's right. Idle hands are the devil's workshop. Work, that's the ticket. You there, young fellow—" He got up and came across the room, pointing a finger at Josh. "You belong to this outfit, eh? Eh?"

90

"Sure he does," said Ted. "He's our foreman."

"Oh, well, in that case, good enough, good enough—"

"Why don't you go see Maureen?" said Ted. "She's in there." He pointed to the kitchen. Old Mr. Arthur nodded vigorously and went back to his chair in front of the terrace as two children came hurtling down the stairs, screaming. At least, the girl, in pursuit of her brother, was screaming like a loon. He, with his arms on his head, was laughing.

Maureen came out of the kitchen shouting, "Cut it out! Pipe down, all of you, or I'll—I'll ram an apple in your mouth!"

"Are there apples?" said Ted.

"No, there are no apples," she snapped. "I just meant— You two! Kevin and Nora! Stop it!" They continued to run around the room, Nora flailing the air in an effort to hit Kevin. "Stop it, I tell you!"

"He called me a mini-monster! He says I come from outdoor space—"

"Outer space, peabrain," said Kevin.

"I hate him!" Nora screamed. "I hate him. I'll hit him, I'll—"

"Will you stop teasing her?" Maureen said sharply to Kevin.

"I notice you don't ask what was she doing to me, do you? Well, I'll tell you what—I was trying to get some shut-eye after being kept up by her and her bellowing all the way from Cleveland, and she sneaked into what's supposed to be my and Teddy's room, isn't it, and yelled *boo* right into my ear—"

"Oh, for goodness sake. Yelled boo. You baby. You stop teasing her, hear? She's tired."

"Well, I'm tired too. You think I like teasing her? It's hard work."

Maureen looked around with an air of desperation, saw Josh and frowned slightly, then shrugged. "Stick around," she said grimly. "It gets worse as it goes on."

8

"So then," Josh said, "I told them how because the house—I told them we call it Tincture of Spain and they thought that was funny—how because it's on the Gulf side where the beach is being shelved away practically inches a day and there used to be a whole house with land and everything in *front* of their house now that disappeared right into the sea so only these foundation stones stick out that you can see at low tide, the zoo got it practically for nothing because even with six bedrooms and iron gates inside the house it won't bring a penny on the market and that's why— Only I didn't tell them about Senator Freebee. I thought maybe they wouldn't be crazy about living where a guy had hung himself—"

"Hanged," said Mrs. Redmond.

"Hung. Hanged. He's dead, and maybe haunts the place, Fat Matt says, and I didn't think they'd want to live where a senator was dangling from the rafters even if he's gone now. I know I wouldn't—"

Mr. Redmond held up his hand. "Josh, take a breath, will you? You are absolutely the only person I've ever known who can talk breathing in and breathing out. Give us a chance to catch up, will you?"

"Catch up with what?"

"With what you're saying, Joshua."

"Well, I'm saying what I'm saying aren't I? What's to catch up? Just listen. I'm telling about the new vet and his family and how they have this dotty old grandfather—"

"Joshua!"

Josh looked at his mother. "What?"

"Never call a person dotty. Never."

"But he is. And that's what Ted called him—"

"Just because a boy is disrespectful to his grandfather doesn't mean—"

"He's not disrespectful at all," Josh said hotly. "He's crazy about the old man. Dotty about him, come to that. They all are. So there."

There was silence at the table. Except, Josh thought, for the sound of chewing. Eating was a funny business all around. Taking this stuff and putting it in a hole in your face and mashing it up and then having it go all the way through and come out the other end. When you thought it over, the whole thing seemed pointless. Of course, some food tasted pretty good, like stone crabs, or clams, but even so—

The idea of bringing this up as a possible topic of discussion crossed his mind and was immediately dismissed. His mother would be bound to say it was not table conversation. He supposed, in fact, it wasn't.

"Joshua," said Mr. Redmond in the patient tone he used to mask irritation, "would you like a Geiger counter?"

"Huh?"

"You're looking at your dinner as if it were possibly radioactive."

"I am?"

"You are. Now what's the trouble? You haven't found an egg in there somewhere, have you?"

"No—I was just thinking about how funny eating is. I mean, you shove all this junk in a hole in your face and mash it up and—"

"Josh!"

"Okay, Mom. I knew you'd want me to stop. Funny thing—I thought I wouldn't say it, about eating, I mean, and then I went ahead and said it anyway. Like I do that a lot, even when I've decided not to."

"You're a blurter," said Mr. Redmond. "I'm not sure it's a condition that's correctable. You might try, of course."

"Sure thing," said Josh cheerfully. And, in fact, he

felt cheerful enough to get on with his now cold dinner. He liked the Arthur family, liked having them so close by, and he thought maybe he could be friends with them. Living here, at Lands End, which was a great place and he loved it, *was* sort of living at land's end. He'd grown up pretty much alone and never had had many friends because of being so far from town or even other houses. Hank Burroughs lived the closest to him, which he supposed was the reason he and Hank were friends at all. Clooney Powers he liked a lot, but Clooney worked just about all the time. The kids at school were friendly enough there, but just about none of them ever got this far down the island. Josh was the first to get on the school bus mornings, the last to leave it afternoons, and his father didn't relish what he called hordes of kids descending on the house, which meant maybe one guy coming to spend the night. Summers, with school out, he spent days without ever seeing anyone his own age.

Yeah, having the Arthurs around was going to be great. He belted down his dessert—gingerbread and whipped cream, and it was good—and stood up.

"I'm going out."

"You're what?" said Mrs. Redmond.

"Mom—I'm going to bike over to the Arthurs'. I told Ted I'd help him get the furniture pushed around and unpack junk and all."

"For someone who reads the encyclopedia so industriously," said Mr. Redmond, "you certainly have a limited vocabulary. *Junk* covers just about everything for you."

Josh bit his lip. The *Encyclopædia Britannica* was beginning to be a monkey on his back in more ways than one. And one of the ways was how it had put him in his father's power over this business of speech. He couldn't even count the number of times his father began a sentence with, "For someone who reads the encyclopedia—" Should've kept his mouth shut about that, all right. Not that he could keep his mouth shut about anything. He wondered if a person could correct a blurting habit. If a person tried, that was. He'd never actually tried. Only thought about it, once in a while, when he'd talked himself into a spot of some kind.

"Well, I don't know," Mrs. Redmond was beginning.

"Mom, it's only seven o'clock. It won't be dark for ages yet. For Pete's sake—"

"Let him go," said Mr. Redmond. "Don't be late getting back, Josh. You know, you really are inconsistent. You're displeased if we don't seem to mind where you are or what you're doing and displeased if we do mind. How are parents supposed to react?"

Josh felt a flash of anger. How did he know how parents were supposed to react? That was their job, to know how to react, wasn't it? Anger always warmed him, made his cheeks flush and his eyes get prickly.

97

Facing his parents now, he could feel the symptoms of an all-out bout of temper, and for the first time that he could ever remember, made a stern and conscious effort to battle it down. He had just enough foresight to realize that if he gave way he'd have to spend the next half hour in yells and accusations, and then put in another hour, practically, getting calmed down by them, and then maybe a half hour of everybody analyzing what his trouble was.

All that would mean he'd be wasting time he could have spent at the Arthurs', and it was at the Arthurs' he wanted to be.

Swallowing hard, he produced a sharklike smile. "Yeah, I guess I am at that. Inconsistent."

He left his parents staring after him.

Dr. Arthur and his father and children were in the huge kitchen, eating at the table with brass legs. They had hot dogs on rolls and cole slaw and some store-bought cake. A carton of milk, a plastic mustard dispenser, and the package of hot dog rolls were in the middle of the table. A radio was playing on the sideboard, which was probably, Josh thought, the reason they hadn't heard him ring the front doorbell. It was playing pretty loud.

Dr. Arthur spied him hovering in the kitchen doorway.

"Hi, there. It's Jim, isn't it?"

"Josh. I rang your bell, but I guess you didn't hear, so I just came in."

"Fine, fine. The doorbell doesn't work, by the way. We found that out. Among the other things that don't work in this house. Six bathrooms and a trickle of water that could scarcely wet a toothbrush."

"And a dishwasher over there," said Maureen, "that made me think at first I'd died and gone to heaven, only it's broken. And only two burners work on the stove. No wonder we can afford the rent."

"Take a seat," said Ted. Josh looked around, finding none to take. "Here, use mine. I'll get this ladder over here—"

"But—"

"Siddown. I'm used to using the stepladder. Maureen, lookit Nora. Look what she's doing."

Nora, tongue showing at the corner of her mouth with the intensity of her concentration, was drawing a picture on the tabletop with a thin brown-gold stream from the mustard dispenser.

"Nora!" Maureen said sharply, causing her sister to clutch the plastic bottle and send a great puddle of mustard oozing over the table. "Nora, what do you think you're doing?"

"Drawing."

"One of these days," said Kevin, "you'll be drawing from behind bars. A preschool delinquent, that's what you are."

"Kevin," said Dr. Arthur, "stop talking like that to your sister."

"Yes, stop talking like that to me!" Nora shrieked. "I hate you, Kev. Hate hate hate hate hate—"

"You sound like a woodpecker. Peck peck peck peck peck—"

"Hate hate hate hate—"

"Stop *yelling!*" Maureen shouted. "You'll get your stomach upset, Nora. And Kevin, you pipe down, hear?"

Nora slid from her chair and sat beating her heels on the floor under the table. When everyone above her, except Kevin, who peered over curiously, simply went on eating, she began to crawl around hitting with a small fist at legs and feet.

Suddenly Maureen yelped, pushed her chair back and leaned over to drag a howling Nora back into view. "You ever bite me again," she said, "and I'll— I'll— Oh, get back in your chair and eat. Blow your nose first."

"She really bite you?" Ted asked.

"A preschool delinquent," Kevin said. "Just like I told you."

Nora, sniffling hugely, glared at him. "I hate you."

"Just don't bite me. Can I have another hot dog, Maureen?"

"If you fix it yourself. You want another one, Dad?"

Dr. Arthur shook his head. During the entire scene

100

he'd been studying a book, and now he glanced up briefly, saying, "Excuse me for reading at the table, but I'm trying to get this by heart by morning."

"What is it, Dad?" Ted asked.

"A prospectus of—"

Old Mr. Arthur, who'd been staring at the wall, suddenly lifted a surprisingly good voice and began to sing. "Speed, bonny boat, like a bird on the wing—"

The rest of the Arthurs, except Maureen, joined in.

" 'Onward!' the sailors cry. 'Carry the lad that's born to be king Over the sea to Skye!' "

Josh looked and listened with a heart-thumping sense of happiness. This table—the food upon it, the behavior around it—was marvelous. Even whining Maureen seemed to him a proper part of the kind of family anyone would delight in. Lots of people talking and shouting and fighting. Even singing.

They were all singing so heartily that at first only Josh observed Nora picking up the mustard again and beginning to squirt it downward onto her hair.

"Hey," he said softly, and Maureen stopped singing abruptly and shouted, "Go into the bathroom this minute and clean yourself up. Now. Beat it!"

Nora, dripping and pungent, looked around the table. "Won't," she said, licking mustard as it trickled down to her mouth.

"Do as your sister says," Dr. Arthur instructed. There was no trace of annoyance or rebuke in his voice, as he went on, "This is ridiculous in a girl all of four years old." He was simply making a comment, and didn't even sound as if he altogether believed it. Maybe, he seemed to imply, it *was* normal behavior for a girl four years old, and if she'd been an animal four years old he'd have known exactly what to expect. His attitude was that a mild reprimand was probably called for, so he made one.

"She's doing it to get attention," said Kevin.

"She's going to get more than she bargained for," Maureen said, "if she doesn't get herself and that slop on the table cleaned up."

Nora stamped down the hall to a bathroom, slammed the door, and beat on it from the inside.

"Is dinner over?" said Ted. "You didn't get any apples."

"I know. I'm sorry." Maureen sighed. "I'll get some tomorrow when I do a proper marketing." She yawned. " 'Scuse me. It's been a long day."

"Oh gosh," said Joshua, jumping up. "I'm sorry. I'll go right away."

"Don't be so touchy," said Maureen. "I didn't mean that. No one ever goes to bed around here until after midnight anyway, no matter what time we get started. I just meant what I said—it's been a long day. Grand-dad?"

"When I was a young lad, before my hair was graaay, stately ships went sailing, sailing o'er the—"

102

"Granddad," Maureen said, lifting her voice above his. "It's been a lovely concert, and now it's time for you to go with Ted. He'll get you tucked in."

"Who are you, my mother?" said the old man.

"No, Granddad, not your mother."

"If you aren't my mother you can't tell me what to do."

"Your mother *said* I could tell you."

"She did, did she?"

"Yes, she did."

"Oh well, then that's all right, that's fair enough."

"Good. Go with Ted, then."

"That one?"

"No, that's Josh. Ted's the one beside him. You remember Ted."

"Ted's mine, isn't he?"

"I sure am, Granddad," said Ted, getting up. "Say good night to everybody and come with me, okay?"

They went up the stairs, the old man holding Ted's hand, Dr. Arthur and Maureen looking after them.

"A vigorous, intelligent, robust man," said Dr. Arthur, "and this is what he comes to."

"He's not all that old, is he?" Josh asked cautiously, not wanting to be personal. His mother and father discouraged personal comments or questions. But he was awfully curious. How did a person *get* arteriosclerosis? "How does a person get arteriosclerosis?"

"By getting older."

"Does everybody get it?" Josh asked nervously.

"If they live long enough. Some people develop it earlier in life than others. My father isn't very old, and I've known people far older who didn't have it. But if a human being lives sufficiently long, he's obliged to get hardening of the arteries."

"Do animals get it?"

"Not all of them."

"But why's that?"

"It's taking a lot of research time to figure that one out. No solid conclusions in yet."

"Animals," said Josh, "never seem to get sick, not the way people do. I mean, when they get sick enough, they die, and until then they're mostly sort of healthy, aren't they?"

"Well, again, we can't be entirely sure. We know that animals in captivity get sick, and we have ways of taking care of them. What an animal in the wild does— if he has, say, a toothache—we suppose he just suffers through it."

Josh, who'd had a toothache once, hunched his shoulders. "Gee, think of an elephant, or a hippo, having a toothache. That'd be horrible."

"Oh, I don't know. Pain's a subjective matter; I imagine a mouse with an impacted molar would suffer quite as much as a giraffe with the same problem. Not that I've ever heard of a mouse with an impacted molar."

Dr. Arthur looked at Kevin, asleep beside his plate,

head cradled on his arms. "I'll carry him up and put him to bed, Maureen. You see what in the world Nora is doing. Probably fallen asleep on the bathroom floor."

Josh saw that it was really time for him to go. Saying good night to Maureen, the only one left in the kitchen to say it to, he made reluctantly for the front door. The great living room was lit only by moonlight falling through the casement windows, and he stopped there a moment, looking at crates and lumpy overstuffed furniture scattered here and there like flotsam. He glanced up the great staircase, where shadows cast by palm fronds and sea grapes moving in the wind seemed to flow up and down, an invasion of dark, flat creatures.

Sighing, he started out.

"Hey," said Ted, coming downstairs two steps at a time like his father. "Hey! I thought you were going to help me unpack."

Happily, Josh turned back.

9

"How're you coming with the encyclopedia?" **Mr.** Redmond asked.

He and Josh were scraping barnacles from the bottom of *Candide*. They'd pulled her onto shore at high tide and now she was braced with ropes and boards, beached but still beautiful, being groomed before high water returned and she was free to float again. They worked quickly to get the scraping done and anti-fouling paint applied before the tide came back.

"I'm not," said Josh. "I quit at D."

"Oh. Why was that?"

"I dunno. There just seem to be so many other things to do."

"Since the Arthurs arrived."

Josh nodded.

This morning his mother had said that they just about never saw him anymore, and his father had said that probably he'd have to work on *Candide* alone, since undoubtedly Josh had plans for spending the day, again, at Tincture of Spain. Josh had hesitated only briefly before shaking his head and saying he'd be glad to help with the boat.

He had expected to go to the Arthurs', as he'd gone every day since they'd first arrived. Once Mrs. Redmond had questioned whether he mightn't wear out his welcome, and Josh had tried to explain how in a family like the Arthurs (not that he thought there was another family like them) you didn't have to worry about things like that. You just sort of got taken in and absorbed and it would be like asking if another bird coming to the feeder would wear out his welcome. The Arthurs accepted everyone, animal or human, that came to their door, and you weren't welcome or not welcome, you were just there.

He thought it would be hard to explain something like this to his own parents, who planned visits and never had unexpected guests.

Still, looking at his father that morning, and realizing with a touch of guilt that he hadn't helped him with *Candide*, or sailed on her, although he'd been invited, since that first day he'd met Ted and the rest of them, he said he'd love to help scrape barnacles and paint, a job he'd always disliked and tried to avoid.

Mr. Redmond had lifted a skeptical brow and said, "Don't go overboard, Joshua. I'm glad to have your help, but not because you're feeling guilty."

"Why should I feel guilty?"

"You shouldn't. Which could have nothing to do with the fact that you do."

The soft, moist Florida air, beaten brassy by the sun, made Josh and his father sweat in rivulets as they worked. Now and then Josh stopped to wipe his forehead with his arm and stare about with a pleased half-smile. The waters of the bay splintered with sunlight. Out of the bayou a flotilla of mergansers came bobbing, looking like bathtub toys. Along the jetty sea gulls rested in a peaceful row. A gang of pelicans sat at the end of the dock, jostling and pushing from time to time, then settling again, like a bunch of restless school kids. In the air, on the water, pelicans were impressive, massy, and powerful. On shore they became sort of scrubby-looking types—so noble at a distance, so saggy-baggy up close. Either way, Josh loved them.

This was the Florida he and his father both preferred, when the winter people, who'd come down for the sun, now fled before it as if running from a conflagration. It left the whole state emptier and therefore nicer. It left Lands End just about deserted, except for the birds, and the porpoises looping lazily into the bay with the tide and then out again with the tide.

Other summers, Josh remembered, working industriously with his scraper, other summers he'd spent just about entirely on his own. The Burroughs family split for Nantucket, Massachusetts, almost as soon as school was out. Clooney could get away occasionally, but mostly worked even harder than he did when school was in. Thinking back now, Josh realized that he'd never really much minded being alone one long summer day after another. He'd take *Scorch* and go over to Catfish Island with lunch and spend hours there, just walking around or sitting very still, feeling like an Indian, as Indian boys his age had wandered over Florida and its islands not so many hundreds of years ago. Maybe even Catfish Island itself, though of that he couldn't be sure. Islands came and islands went.

"What island?" Ted had asked late yesterday afternoon.

"That one," Josh had said, pointing. "Right out there in the bay." It wasn't half a mile out from Lands End, and was less than a quarter of a mile long and even less than that wide. "It's one of my favorite places in the world," Josh had said.

Ted had laughed. "How many places in the world have you seen?"

"Not many," Josh had said tranquilly. "That one's still one of my favorites."

"Is it inhabited?"

"Not by people. What my father's scared of is that somebody'll get up enough money to buy it and turn it into some goddam development. We could've, I mean my father could've, bought it for maybe twenty-five thousand dollars about ten years ago, only we didn't have twenty-five thousand dollars. Now he says he could just manage that, but now it costs seventy-five thousand. I'm going to make a bomb and blow the whole thing up if somebody buys it for a development."

Ted had looked only mildly interested in the bombing project, but had said he'd sure like to see the island before it went up in smoke.

"I'll take you over in *Scorch* one day. Or the canoe."

"When?"

"Tomorrow, if you want. If there's any wind. Or if you don't mind paddling if there isn't any wind."

"I don't mind. I'd like it."

And then, this morning, he'd been obliged, by his own sense of guilt, which his father correctly said he felt whether or not he should feel it, to agree to this job on *Candide*. Well, if they worked fast, maybe he'd be done in time to get over to Ted's by late morning or early afternoon.

"What's it inhabited by?" Ted had asked.

"Birds. Snakes. Raccoons. There's an owl over there thinks he owns the place. A barn owl."

"No kidding." Ted had looked elated. "I've practically never seen a wild animal."

"What do you mean? You see them all the time. You even get to live with them."

"I mean wild in the wild. In Cleveland I think the animals inside sort of scared off outside things, like raccoons. No raccoon wants to tangle with a lion, even if he's never heard about lions. He just knows better."

"That jaguar at the zoo," Josh said to his father now, "that one that's going to have babies. Dr. Arthur says he'll probably have to take the babies away because she's so mean she probably won't nurse them. He says you can tell by an animal's eyes if it was captured in the wild or was born and raised in a zoo. He says that jaguar, Fatima her name is, has never resigned herself to captivity, the way the cheetahs apparently have. You know, he can go right in the enclosure with the cheetahs and they go up to him if he has food for them or even if he hasn't. Even Dr. Claven never got them to do that, Fat Matt says."

"Your friend Dr. Arthur sounds like quite a fellow."

"Yeah." He didn't add that he sometimes got the feeling that he'd have been more welcome around Dr. Arthur if he'd been a warthog. No, more welcome wasn't what he meant. He got the feeling that Dr. Arthur felt sure of himself with animals but hadn't quite decided what people, including his own children, were about.

"We're looking forward to meeting them all sometime."

Josh didn't reply to that at all. Over a month now the Arthurs had been here, but his mother had so much

111

committee work and his father was so averse to having his time taken up that it had never occurred to them to invite the Arthurs over for a meal, or even a visit in the afternoon.

"People these days are so wasteful," his father sometimes said. "Waste water, timber, minerals. Waste lives, love. Waste time. Toss hours away, as if hours were redeemable, looking at drivel on television or being with people they don't care about and calling it 'entertaining.' And for what? To be sociable? To get away from themselves and their own thoughts? I really can't figure it out. But for my part, I do not intend to waste one minute of my life if I can help it."

Wasting time, according to his father and apparently to his mother, too—at least, she went along—was what you did when you went out for dinner or had someone in. His parents had just about no social life at all, and had looked surprised when he asked if they could invite the Arthurs for dinner.

"Why, dear?" Mrs. Redmond had asked. "We've never had the Burroughses for dinner, or Clooney's parents. You've never asked us to ask them."

"Well, the Arthurs are different," he'd said moodily.

"All right then, Josh, we'll have them some evening."

But the plan had never been mentioned again and Josh thought his mother had probably quite honestly forgotten.

Josh, on the other hand, had eaten at the Arthurs'

so often that he'd lost track of how many times. His parents objected, saying he was taking advantage of easygoing people, but since they hadn't met the easygoing people they had no way of knowing at all. He probably, he thought, could move in at Tincture of Spain and no one would object. It would probably take them quite a while even to notice.

Because he ate there so much, his mother had taken to sending things over. Bread and pies when she baked. A big pot of stew or vegetable soup. His mother could cook. There was no way of knowing whether Maureen could, since she never did. She just opened packages and cans. The Arthur kids were always glad to have what his mother sent around, because Dr. Arthur was absentminded and sometimes forgot to give Maureen marketing money. Days went by when he just about didn't appear home at all, and it was Maureen and Ted who'd got them all entered in school for the fall, who did the cooking—such as it was—and the housecleaning —as much as it got cleaned, which wasn't much. They were the ones who looked after the younger children and the old man.

Josh, who got an early start mornings because of his mother's insistence that the three of them have breakfast together before his father left for work at seven, had arrived at the Arthurs' the day before to find Maureen and Ted and Nora still at their breakfast. Dr. Arthur was gone, but he always left even earlier than

113

Mr. Redmond did. Mr. Arthur was in his chair on the terrace, tapping his hands on his knees and staring out to sea.

The table was still littered, and Josh saw they'd had hot dogs for breakfast. What a dandy way to live. "Can I have some coffee?" he asked happily.

"Sure," said Maureen. "There's some instant somewhere in that mess on the sideboard."

"Do you ever have to eat eggs?" Josh asked while he waited for the kettle to whistle. "I mean, I never get hot dogs for breakfast, and I have to eat an egg twice a week. Sometimes I won't, and then I have to throw my whole breakfast out to the gulls."

"We don't *have* to eat them," Maureen said. "We do, sometimes. I like them."

"I hate them," Josh said, sitting down with his coffee.

"Maybe because you're so crazy about birds," Ted suggested. "You feel like a cannibal, eating an egg."

"I'm not crazy about chickens," Josh pointed out, interested in Ted's theory.

"An egg's an egg, and comes from a bird. That's probably your hang-up."

Josh sipped coffee and turned this new idea over in his mind.

"Where's Kevin?" Maureen said suddenly.

"I don't know," said her brother.

"What do you mean, you don't know?"

"I mean that to me Kevin's whereabouts are a mystery. An unfathomable myst—"

114

"Oh, *Ted*. Can't you help me just a little bit with the children? Is it your whole aim in life just to make wisecracks?" she asked, sort of unfairly, Josh thought. Ted helped loads.

"Actually," Ted answered, "I was thinking of carving out a career in the space program."

"Well, you ought to be comfortable there. You're spacey enough."

Ted and Josh had exchanged glances, and just then Kevin wandered in. He had mud on his shoes, on his pants and shirt, on his face, and in his hair. He was picking his nose in a rapt and pensive manner.

"Kevin!"

He looked at Maureen, his hand falling. "Huh?"

"Where have you been?"

"Playing."

"In a sewer?"

Kevin looked down at himself. "No. Just around."

"Go upstairs this minute and take a shower."

Kevin sat down. "I had a shower."

"You had one exactly a week ago. I've been keeping track. And I've been watching the laundry, too. You haven't changed your shirt or underwear since you *took* that shower. I wasn't going to say anything. I was going to wait until you couldn't stand yourself, but apparently you can outlast me, so I'm *telling* you—change your underwear and your shirt."

"I can't change my shirt. I only have one other one, and Ted used it for a rag."

"Oh, for the— Ted, why did you do that?"

"Because it was a rag."

"Sometimes," Maureen said slowly, "sometimes I think I'll just go someplace and crack up."

"When?" Kevin asked curiously.

"Will you kindly go and take a shower?"

"I don't want to. What's the point in taking a shower? I just get dirty again."

"You might as well ask what's the point in eating, you just get hungry again."

"I am hungry again. Can I have some Product 19?"

Maureen started from her chair and Kevin ran for the stairs, shouting over his shoulder, "You're a pain in the neck, Maureen! A great big blasted pain in the neck!" Nora trailed after him.

Sinking back, Maureen sighed and shook her head. "Was I too hard on him?" she asked Ted.

"Nah. Anyway, even if you were he wouldn't notice probably. Kevin lives in a world inhabited by Kevin alone. What anybody else is doing or feeling or saying doesn't get through. He's just making noises."

Maureen sighed.

Nora came back down and said importantly, "Kevin says not to interrupt him, he'll be back as soon as he's finished shaving."

"Shaving?" Maureen frowned. "What's he shaving, the bathmat?"

"His eyebrows."

"Nora, that's a silly thing to say. Not funny at all."

"I think it's gonna look very funny. He's already got one off."

"You mean to tell us he's actually shaving his eyebrows?"

"That's what I *been* telling you."

Maureen stared at Ted. "What are we going to do?"

"Search me. Maybe I better go take a look. Probably he doesn't have a blade in the razor—"

"Yes, he does," said Nora.

Kevin, still mostly mud-covered, sidled down the stairs, tears streaming down his startlingly clean face.

"Lookit me," he said shakily.

His face, denuded of eyebrows, had taken on a strangely egglike appearance.

"Lookit me, Maureen," he said and began to choke with great hiccuping sobs.

Nora shrieked, pointing at him. "He's horrible, he's awful! I'm not gonna talk to him, ever. He looks like a—"

"Shut up," said Maureen. She pulled Kevin against her, holding him in her arms. "They'll grow back, honey. It won't take too long. Do you want me to put eyebrow pencil on you?"

Kevin wailed, shaking his head against her shoulder. Old Mr. Arthur came from the terrace and said nervously, "Somebody's making a bad noise someplace. What's that noise? Tell whoever that is to stop or I'll call the cops. Fine thing, making a noise like that in the middle of the day. I want that to stop—"

Ted got up. "Josh, would you like to take Granddad for a walk on the beach with me? It's time for his walk."

On the whole, Josh thought now, putting aside his scraper and going for the anti-fouling paint, on the whole he'd just as soon give this whole family jazz a miss when he grew up. He'd be an adventurer, unencumbered, roving the wild spaces of the world if he could find any. Maybe Ted Arthur could go with him. He imagined Ted would've had a bellyful of family life by the time he got to be an adult. Maybe the two of them could build a boat together and go around the world like Sir Francis Chichester. They could name their boat *Lands End*, meaning all sorts of things. That the end of the land had been reached, that they'd left all land behind them, that—

"You want to go out with me this afternoon?" Mr. Redmond was asking.

Josh emerged from his reverie and looked at his father in consternation. "Yeah, of course, Dad. I mean— yeah, sure."

"What you mean is not *yeah, sure*, but that you had something else in mind."

"No, really—"

"Josh, when will you learn to be honest with people?"

"I am honest! What d'ya mean, honest? I don't lie—"
Much, he added to himself.

118

"I mean honest about your feelings. Direct. Why can't you just tell me that you have something else you want to do? If you'd think a little ahead, you'd realize that the two of us sailing together when you'd rather be doing something else isn't going to be precisely a pick-me-up for either of us. I've tried and tried to get you to understand that the only way to deal with people is directly. Say what you mean, what you think."

"Half the time if I say what I think, Mom tells me I'm being rude."

"Joshua, don't fence with me. You know what I mean."

Well, but I don't, thought Josh. I just about never know what you mean. "Besides, I would like to go with you. It's just—I sort of told Ted I'd take him over to Catfish Island. Maybe we could take Ted with us, huh? He's never been on a sailboat," Josh explained, a pitying note in his voice.

"Oh—well, of course, fine. That'd be fine," said Mr. Redmond.

Now who isn't being direct? Josh thought. Being in the confined quarters of even as big a boat as *Candide* with a stranger, especially a stranger who was also a kid, wasn't his father's bag, no way. But did he come right out and say it? He did not. It was okay to tell people to be direct in their dealings with others, but when you came right down to it, who was? Hank Burroughs' father, when he was boiled, that's who was.

Mr. Burroughs went around insulting people all over the place, giving his honest views that he wouldn't think of giving when he was sober. Nora Arthur, four years old. She was another one who went around saying what she thought, and usually ended by getting somebody, or everybody, furious with her.

The other day, when they'd all been trying to clean up trash washed onto the beach by a very high tide, Mrs. Claven had come by to say hello and see how things were going, and Nora had looked at her and said, "She's so *wrinkled*, Maureen. Why isn't she in the sky instead of Momma?" Mrs. Claven had tried to laugh it off, and Maureen had stuttered trying to smooth out Nora's meaning, or make it sound like some other meaning, but it had sure been a mess, and Maureen hadn't got over it yet.

No, the way Josh saw it, being honest and direct— which wasn't in his opinion the same thing as not telling lies unless you absolutely had to—often led to trouble instead of the other way around.

He considered saying something to his father like, "Lookit, you'd rather sail alone, and Ted and I want to see the island, so why don't we all just do what we want to do?"

Somehow he couldn't make himself say it.

And then when they'd finished applying the anti-fouling paint, his father got a call from the chandlery and had to drop everything and go into town. Josh

120

wished he'd more wholeheartedly agreed to go now that he didn't have to. But still he was relieved not to have to take Ted on *Candide* with his father being too polite one minute and absentminded the next, as if he and Ted weren't there at all. So Josh decided he'd go on *not* saying what he meant unless what he meant was clearly what somebody else wanted to hear. He got in enough trouble talking as it was, without adding the complication of candor.

10

Just before noon, he and Ted, with a lunch of peanut butter sandwiches, apples, and milk in a thermos bottle, took off for Catfish Island in *Scorch*. The wind was so good that they were there before Josh had had time to explain even a simple term like reefing. Dropping his sail in good time, he ran *Scorch* into shallow water, and together they beached her.

"We'd better eat lunch now," Josh said. "If we leave it here the raccoons or the sea gulls or *something* will be bound to get it."

They sat cross-legged on the sand, on the farther side of the island, munching peacefully and gazing over the blue sun-burnished bay. Out there skiffs and rowboats and big power boats rode at anchor, and men with poles and bait and hooks and nets fished with the seemingly inexhaustible patience of fishermen. And birds, without the benefit of lures, were going about their own ceaseless job of fishing.

Cormorants shot into the water like dark bullets and disappeared, to emerge moments later, yards away, sometimes with a catch, sometimes without.

"Do they catch their fish *underwater?*" Ted asked.

"A cormorant can outswim most fish, believe it or not. Anhingas, too. Not like pelicans. Pelicans just dive in and come right up again. Watch that one—"

A brown pelican flew past, suddenly angled his great wings backward like elbows, peeled off, and dove for the water, hitting with a solid splash. As he went, a sea gull slid into place above him, hovered until the pelican surfaced, and landed on the big bird's head. The pelican pressed his pouch against his chest, then tossed his head back and gulped while the sea gull jabbed at a disappearing fishtail.

Ted laughed. "Did you see that?"

"Sea gulls do it all the time. They're trying to confuse the pelican so much that he loses his fish. And pretty often they do. Pelicans," Josh said fondly, "are sort of easily confused."

"How can a sea gull get a fish that's in that big pouch?"

"Well, the difficulty is that when the pelican grabs the fish he also gets a mouthful—and what a mouthful—of water. That's why he pushes his pouch against

123

his chest, to expel the water. But he has to open his mouth to expel it and that's when the sea gull moves in. I've seen one stick his head right into a pelican's mouth and pull the fish out. The gall of a gull is something else. Especially laughing gulls. That was a laughing gull just now, the kind that look like they have black stocking masks on, with white lines around their eyes. Herring gulls aren't so bad. Or maybe it's just because they're too big to land on the pelican's head. But pelicans," he went on happily, finding in Ted the kind of audience he'd always known must exist, the kind that *wanted* him to share and explain things, "are very dignified creatures. I've seen a flock of gulls gang up on a single pelican like a bunch of hoods, but I've never seen a pelican fight back. He just patiently outwaits them."

"Maybe he's a coward."

"Pelicans are *not* cowards. They're above brawling, is all."

When they'd finished with lunch and put the thermos and paper bags in the boat, Ted lay back on the sand, hands behind his head, and said, "Boy, what a neat place."

Josh looked around, trying to see the island through new eyes, though his old ones had always regarded it as perfect. The pale fine sand of the beach was strewn with driftwood washed there by countless tides. Behind them sea oats waved slenderly, behind the sea oats the mangroves grew, and in back of them Australian pines were thick and tall and plumey to the other shore.

If anybody ever buys it and makes a development out of it, Josh thought desperately, I'll—I'll—leave Lands End. If he ever had to look across and see this island with houses squashed on quarter-acre lots and the trees down, television antennas spiking up, and people all over it, he might as well go and live in Tallahassee.

"I guess you're the luckiest guy I ever met," Ted said drowsily.

Josh looked over at him. "I sometimes think that about you."

Ted appeared perplexed, then said, "Oh, you mean the animals, getting to keep them at home. Well, that's great, all right. But you know, I sometimes think there's gotta be something in life besides lions tearing up the furniture. Like your room," he went on, "that time I went in with you for a minute—"

Josh frowned. Ted didn't seem to be being sarcastic, but the fact was he had only been in Josh's house once, for a few minutes while Josh got into his trunks so they could go swimming. Dandy way to treat a friend, Josh thought now. Just jim-dandy.

Ted had walked around his room that day, admiring just about everything. The ship models that Josh had made and kept on shelves, his collection of sea stuff— conch shells, dried sea urchins, starfish and sea horses and sand dollars. He'd especially liked the long row of sand dollars, ranging from little ones smaller than a dime up to one that was nearly five inches across. They came in all shades, from almost black to the bleachedest white. Josh liked sand dollars, the way they looked.

"It's like a little starfish, there in the center," Ted had said, turning one carefully in his hand.

"A sand dollar is a starfish. Echinoderms, they're called. When we were kids we used to skim live ones at each other. Live sand dollars have this sharp ridge all the way around. We used to have a war game with them—the guy who got the most cuts lost."

"How do they swim, with all that sandy shell around them?"

"Actually, they're sort of helpless, and they don't swim much because they live buried in the sand. They have these little tiny tiny feet and can get around. But the point is, nothing really preys on them because nothing wants to eat them. I guess they just die and then the tide washes them up on the beach, or the tide washes them up on the beach and they die. Either way. I quit playing that game with them because they didn't seem to have a chance, you know. No way of protecting themselves. Seems funny, I suppose, to feel sorry for a sand dollar that I guess doesn't have much feelings of its own, but that's how it took me."

"I don't think it's funny," Ted had said, putting the sand dollar carefully back in place and wandering around the room again, looking at books, at pictures, at the mullet net that Josh had for a curtain at his window, at an old horseshoe-crab shell, the back part, that Josh had worn for a helmet in a school play when he'd been seven.

"I'd like to have a room like yours," Ted said now. "Bed all made up, and a real chair with cushions that the stuffing isn't squeezing out of. And that desk. That's sure a neat desk. All those shells and things. It's great. In our house—anyplace we live—I don't think the beds are made except the day Maureen and I change the sheets. I mean, even when Mom was alive—even then the beds never got made, and the insides were always flying out of the sofa. You know how it looks at the Arthur household. I just think it'd be nice, sometime, to live neat. Neatly. The way your folks do."

Easy enough to be neat if there's never anybody or anything around to unneaten things, Josh thought. He said, "Do you think—hey, Ted, I got this great idea. Do you suppose we could talk them into letting us switch? For a while, I mean. Not forever." He sat up excitedly. "What d'ya think?"

"Switch?" Ted looked puzzled. "You mean—I go live at your house and you live at mine?"

"Yeah. What d'ya suppose? Would they? Let us, I mean?"

Ted was staring at Josh as if he'd suddenly gone crazy. He frowned, not saying anything, and then, scratching his chin, mused, "I dunno. I just don't. I mean, I suppose we could put you in my house all right. They maybe, except Maureen, wouldn't ever notice the difference—"

"Your grandfather would. He's crazy about you."

"No, he wouldn't care. Not if you were nice to him. That's all Granddad needs, somebody being kind to him. Taking care of him, of course." Ted sighed. "You see, it wouldn't work. You wouldn't know how to take care of him."

"I get along with him fine," Josh said indignantly.

"Getting along is one thing, taking care is another. Like, I give him his bath, every other night—every night'd be too much for both of us. You gotta know things like he's scared to get down in the tub in water. I've got this rubber hose with a spray at the end, and Granddad just stands in the tub, like a horse, and I wash him down. You couldn't do that."

"Why not?"

Ted studied him. "Would you?"

"Sure I would. What d'ya think I am, a dope, that I couldn't wash an old man down with a hose?"

"I just thought you might not *want* to."

"I wouldn't mind. Is your father really going to bring the baby jaguars home?"

"Oh, that's it, huh?"

"That's partly it," Josh said impatiently. "Not all of it. Sure I'd like to be in on the bringing up of baby jaguars, but that's not *all* why I'd like to switch."

128

Ted sighed. "I'd like to be out of it, for once."

"Well then, what about it? Shall we ask them?"

"It's okay with me," Ted said slowly. "I just don't think—oh, come off it, Josh. Your parents would think we'd both lost our marbles. Nah, they'd never do it." He jumped up. "Let's walk around this island of yours, okay?"

Josh got to his feet more slowly and stood for another while looking across the water toward his own house. *Candide*, he saw, was gone from her mooring. So his father had settled whatever it was at the chandlery and had dashed back to his love, his sloop. From here, Josh could see that his mother's car was gone, so she was off somewhere steering some youth back onto the right track, or listening to the history of the hibiscus at the Garden Club, or—whatever.

As if he could see through the walls, he knew how the inside of the house was now. Neat and nice-smelling, with the grandfather clock's *tick-tock* sedate in the silence. Probably something his mother had baked set carefully on the sideboard for dinner. Undisturbed and quiet, quiet, except for the clock.

"Where's Momma?" Nora had said the other day, her voice high in panic. "I want my Momma!"

She often did that. Suddenly and without warning she'd cry out for her mother.

Kevin had answered, as he usually did, "She's in the sky."

"What's up there?" Nora wailed.

"A big farm," Kevin said firmly. "Lots and lots of animals."

Nora had subsided, and that, too, was the way it usually went. She'd sniffled and said, "Momma's helping to take care of them?"

"Yes. They need her." As Nora had showed signs of renewed anger, or pain—it was hard to tell which she felt most—Kevin had added hastily, "They need her more than we do, Nora. We've got Maureen and Ted and Dad and Granddad—"

"That's right, that's right," the old man had said. "Now you've got it. All those people they're pretty well halfway, you know, but we didn't come here to hurt them—"

"No, we didn't, Granddad," Ted had said. "We're peaceable."

"Of course we are. Just the same, I'm going to let that one have it right in the kisser if he doesn't stop marching around that way, that one over there, you see him don't you—"

"He's gone now, Granddad. He said he had to leave."

"Oh, he did, did he. Well, he knows which side is up all right. That's a good one, that is." The old man had slapped his thigh and given his deep, hearty laugh. "If he comes back, just leave it to me, that's all, I'll let him have one right in the—"

A funny, ramshackle, kind of loco household, Josh admitted to himself, and if his mother ever got around to visiting, which he was thankfully pretty sure she wouldn't, she'd probably say it called for action on the part of the authorities. She'd say it was insanitary, dietetically unsound, that the kids were neglected and overworked, the old man half-mad and the father irresponsible. She'd say that something should be done about it. Being his mother, she might even try to do the something. Which would be awful, and the end of that friendship, all right.

Relinquishing the idea of even a temporary switch (one of his nuttier ideas, he decided) Josh said, "Want to explore? There's a place where the owl drops the skeletons of snakes, and sometimes you can get practically a whole one. You ever see a snake skeleton? They're really pretty. Awfully fragile. Look sort of like white ferns. And over on the other side is the place I usually see the raccoon, way up in the crotch of a tree sleeping away like a baby bear, and if we're very quiet we can maybe see the owl—"

"How can we be quiet if you keep talking all the time?" Ted asked, not in the least unpleasantly. He posed it as a question to be answered.

Josh stopped walking. "You really think I talk too much, huh?"

Ted shrugged. "I didn't say that. I didn't say *too much*. I just said—but since you ask, you do talk an awful lot."

"Well, but—" Josh pushed his hand through his hair.

131

"How're you—how's a person going to have conversations, and share things and all, if they don't talk?"

"I got nothing against sharing things and talking. I think it's great. And lots of the stuff you tell is really interesting. It's just—well, nobody wants to just listen all the time, you know. You practically never give the other person part of the sharing, if you follow me."

"Oh, I follow you all right. You laid a very clear trail."

They walked on in silence for a long time, and then Ted said, "You sore?"

"No," said Josh, telling the truth. "I was just thinking about what you said." The way Ted put things, you couldn't get sore at him. It wasn't like his parents, always yakking at him about yakking. Ted had just been telling him a fact.

Come to that, he supposed his parents had just been telling him a fact, too. Funny it should sound so different, coming from Ted.

"No," he said again. "I'm not sore."

"Let's find the snake skeletons," Ted said. "Let's see if we can find those."

11

Dr. Arthur's prediction about the maternal instincts of Fatima, the mother jaguar, proved correct. She had one kitten and tried to kill it.

"For about ten minutes," he told his children and Josh, "we thought maybe motherhood would win out. She bit off the umbilical cord and began to lick the kitten; then all at once she snarled and started to cuff the little thing around. Good thing we were there."

"Who's we?" Josh asked.

"One of the college kids who works at the zoo on her holidays was with me. Clara. Nice girl. She's going to be a vet herself."

"And she gets to help out with the animals?" Josh asked. "Helps them get born and all?"

"I'll tell you, Josh. She does a lot more cleaning out

of cages than anything else. As in other lines of work, you have to start at the bottom of the zoo."

"I've seen her," said Maureen. "She's pretty."

"A nice girl."

"You've already said that," Maureen snapped.

"Well? No harm done."

Maureen eyed her father as if she had more to say, but only asked where the jaguar was now.

"In the zoo nursery," Dr. Arthur replied. "But if it's okay with you kids, I'll bring her home in a couple of weeks. Don't want to leave her in a cage longer than it's necessary."

"Why's it necessary now?" Ted demanded. "We took the lion cubs the first day."

"That was when—when your mother was with us, Ted. She had the time—anyway, took the time—to feed them every couple of hours around the clock for a month. We aren't set up for that now. It's hard enough on Maureen having to do all she has to do without adding Cleo to her burdens."

"Cleo?" said Maureen. "You've already named her, without asking us?"

"Oh, knock it off, Maureen. What's wrong with you? The kitten was there and we needed a name for her so we gave her one."

"You and Clara, you mean. You gave her one, the two of you."

Dr. Arthur got up and walked out of the house. They

heard the sound of the van backing up and then rattling off in the direction of the zoo.

"What the heck's eating you, Maureen?" Ted asked his sister. "Why're you so crabby?"

"Well, if you can't figure it out, I'm not going to enlighten you."

Ted's mouth dropped open. "Oh boy," he breathed. "Oh man, are you flakey. Dad says one nice word about —about a member of the opposite sex, and you take a broad jump into him getting married." He turned to Josh. "She's been like this ever since—I mean every time Dad *mentions* a woman's name. And the last one, you remember, Maureen, that he said was nice, that lady in the zoology department, she turned out to be about eighty years old. Besides, she *was* nice. Besides, if this girl's in college, she'd be maybe a little young for Dad, huh? Like the zoology professor was too old?"

"Our father, in case you hadn't noticed, is a very youthful and attractive man, and any woman or girl would be lucky to—"

"Knock it off," said Ted, in imitation of his father. "You give me a bellyache, Maureen."

Her eyes filling with tears, Maureen went up the broad staircase, walking in the center, her arms hanging beside her, looking tragic.

Her brother stared after her. "Wow." He turned to Josh. "That's the way it's getting to be around our house all the time. Everybody jumpy as a pondful of frogs, and

135

Dad might as well sleep in one of the cages himself, for all we ever see of him. The only one who seems okay is Granddad."

"And you," said Josh. "You seem okay, too."

Ted shrugged. "I don't count me. I have no imagination and no intuition and no insight and no a lot of other things and it comes out to I'm okay the way fools are okay. They don't know any better."

It was clear that he was quoting Maureen, but Josh didn't want to get into it. He said, "Could we go over and see the jaguar? The baby?"

"They won't let us in the nursery. We could contaminate the animals."

Maureen came downstairs with Nora and Kevin and said, "I told the children we'd take them to the zoo. Maybe they can look at their Poppa through the window, or the bars, so as to remember what he looks like. I think it's so nice for children to have some general idea of Daddy's appearance."

"You can take them by yourself, if that's how it's going to be," said Ted. "You're in one of your moods, and I don't want any part of it."

Maureen stiffened, then let her shoulders slump. "Oh well," she said. "I don't care. I'll take them by myself."

Old Mr. Arthur, beret neatly centered, came out of the kitchen shadowboxing. "There, there and *there*," he said, feinting at the air. "Teach you manners, you young cub. That's the stuff, that's the stuff. Give it to him—"

"Granddad," said Ted, taking the old man's hands, "they've gone now. You don't have to fight them anymore."

"That a fact?"

"Fact."

"Well, what now, what now? Who are the rest of these people?"

"You know who they are, Granddad. You're just kidding us."

The old man laughed. "I do, eh? Well, that's good enough."

"We're all going to the zoo, for a trip," said Ted. Maureen looked at him with no change in expression, and he went on, "A nice little walk in the hot sun and when we get there we can look at the animals and have some ice cream."

"I want ice cream first," said Nora.

"What you'll get is a poke in the snoot," said old Mr. Arthur, and Ted burst out laughing as Maureen frowned and said, "Now, Granddad, you don't want to talk to Nora that way."

"No," he said gravely. "No, indeed. She's a nice little girl. *Girl*," he said, glaring at Nora, who stuck her tongue out at him.

"Oh boy," said Ted. "Even Granddad's caught it." But he was still half laughing. "What a bunch of nuts."

Kevin said, "We really gonna go to the zoo, Teddy? Could we see the baby jag?"

"You know better than that, Kev. We can't get in the

nursery. But we could look at the other animals. Anyway, it's something to do, all of us. Want to come along, Josh?"

Josh did want to. The six of them set out to walk the mile to the zoo. Ted and Josh together could have taken a shortcut through the mangrove swamps, across the sandflats, and through a palm grove behind the zoo. But with Nora and old Mr. Arthur along they went the long way around by the streets. Mr. Arthur talked and sang in a loud voice all the way. Passersby stared and smiled, or stared and looked quickly away. Maureen's cheeks became a bit flushed, but other than that the Arthurs paid no attention to the attention they attracted.

"This is nothing," Ted said once. "You should be with us when we have aardvarks on our tail."

Josh had to laugh. "Do you use leashes for them?"

"Not always. They get so affectionate that they follow like dogs, but sometimes we use leashes just so people won't panic. You'd be surprised at how many dopes get frightened just seeing an aardvark or a lion that's loose. And if the people get scared and squawk or something, it's apt to scare the animals. The leashes are really protection for the animals."

"Except for peccaries," Maureen said. The walk, and the prospect of being out of the house for a while, seemed to have restored her spirits. Although she still complained bitterly from time to time about the heat and humidity, today she swung along, nose in the air,

138

looking happy and competent, with Nora hanging onto one hand and her grandfather clutching the other.

"Peccaries," she said, "go about in the wild with their snouts pushed right against their mother's side, and if they don't have a mother's side to push against, they'll use whatever they can for a substitute. In our case, it was always somebody's legs, because that's as high as they can reach. My mother had permanent dents in the calves of her legs from peccaries nuzzling her everywhere she went. You don't need a leash for a peccary because it wouldn't take its nose off you for *any* reason."

Josh was always amazed at how casually these kids assumed that wild animals were a normal part of everyday life, whereas the things that other people—his mother, for example—considered normal—regular mealtimes, real furniture, stuff like that—seemed to the Arthurs just beside the point. At Tincture of Spain, several crates were still untouched since the day they'd been put in, and when Josh had offered to help unpack them, Maureen had said she thought they wouldn't bother. "We've forgotten what's in them, so I guess we don't need any of it," she'd said, and now they used the crates for piling other stuff on. Mrs. Redmond would have found this incredible if she'd known about it. But she'd have found the entire setup incredible, and Josh had given up asking for the Arthurs to be invited for a meal, and could only sigh with relief that his parents were apparently never going to get around to it.

139

Just inside the zoo entrance was the man-made lake with the ducks that could fly away and the flamingos that could not. Mr. Arthur stopped short when he saw it.

"Now, look at that, will you," he said. "Look at all those big chickens."

"Aren't they something, Granddad?" said Kevin.

"Cluck, cluck, cluck, cluuck—"

"Not so loud, Granddad," said Maureen. "You'll frighten them."

"Oh." The old man looked thoughtful, then lowered his voice and continued to cluck as they walked on in the hot, moist air, heavy with the scent of caged wild animals.

"I'm thursday," Nora whined.

"Thirsty," Maureen corrected absently.

"Me too," said Kevin. "I'm thursday too."

"Oh, Kev." Maureen smiled. "Okay, we'll go get something to—"

"I want somethin' to eat, too!" Nora yelled. "You didn't give me nuthin' to eat all day!"

"Stop yelling, will you? You're attracting attention."

"I don't care about attention. I wanna hodog anna Coke anna—"

"Shut up," Maureen said fiercely. "Stop that shouting—"

"What's all this noise?" old Mr. Arthur said nervously. "There's an awful lot of noise around here. I think we better get out of here before it happens."

140

"Now see what you've done, you little pest," Maureen said, at the same time as Ted leaned over and said, "One more peep out of you, Nora, and I'm going to take you home and leave everybody else here to have the fun."

"What fun?" Nora mumbled, but she quieted down nevertheless.

Josh felt sorry for her. She was sort of whiney and sort of a pest. She was also very small, and he wouldn't have been surprised if she had been telling the truth about not having had anything to eat. The Arthurs seemed to forget to eat, except odd things at odd times. Maybe she *was* hungry and thursday.

Maureen, with Kevin, strode ahead of her family into the zoo cafeteria and said to Ted, "Why don't you and Josh keep Granddad and Nora here. Take that table over there and lean the other two chairs against it for Kev and me. We'll get something for—"

"I wanna go up to the place and pick my own!" Nora shouted. "I wanna pick my own!"

"Oh, for the love of—all right, all right. You all go up, and I'll sit here with Granddad. Here's the change purse, Ted. And remember, that's all the money we have until Friday."

"I don't wanna go with Ted," Nora yelled. "I want you to come with me. He pinches me and doesn't let me have nuthin'."

"I do not—" Ted began, as Maureen said, "The next time you get taken out, Nora-bora, it's going to be on a leash *with* a muzzle. Now, cut it out. You're upsetting Granddad."

"Just the same, you come with me. Or I won't go."

"Look," Maureen said in a level, menacing tone, "you sit down, *now*. Stay there with Granddad. Ted, stay with them, will you? I'll take Kev and Josh and get us some sort of slop. This is some fun-filled expedition."

"I don't wanna stay with—" Nora began, and sat down, her lip quivering.

Maureen, abruptly changing tactics, said, "That's a good girl. We'll get you a balloon later, okay?"

On the cafeteria line, Kevin, who never moved quickly, hesitated before reaching for his hot dog when it was put on the counter. An unshaven man in workman's clothes reached for it, then turned in surprise when Maureen snapped, "That isn't yours, and don't you touch it!"

"Huh?"

"You heard me. That's not your hot dog."

"Yeah? Whose was it?"

"Not was. Is. It's my brother's. Keep your dirty hands off it."

"Just who the hell do you think you are, sister?" the man demanded. By now everyone's attention was on them, most beholders delighted at the diversion. Josh and Kevin were not delighted. They were scarlet with mortification.

"Who the hell do you think *you* are?" Maureen asked. "Grabbing a little boy's hot dog!"

"I take care of number one, sister. That's my philosophy."

Maureen looked him up and down. "We can see," she sneered, "that your philosophy has taken you a long way in life."

Suddenly the man snorted. "You're nuts. A real nut case. Here, sonny, take your hot dog. Probably a cold dog by now."

"Don't take it," Maureen began. "We'll get you a hot one—"

But Kevin had already seized the paper plate with the disputed hot dog and was lining up for French fries, trying to put distance between himself and his sister.

"What was that all about?" Ted asked, when they were at length seated at the round, rusty iron table with hot dogs, pizza slices, French fries, and Cokes sorted out among them.

"I don't know what it was about. Fair play, maybe." Maureen leaned her elbows on the table and stared toward the flamingos.

"Aren't you going to eat your pizza?" Ted asked after a bit.

"Nope."

"Can I—"

"Help yourself."

"Who're all these people?" old Mr. Arthur asked plaintively. "I don't want all these people, tell them to go away."

"If only we could," Maureen said, smiling at him

mournfully. "But it's all right, Granddad. Don't worry. They can't bother you."

"I want my balloon!" Nora said shrilly. "And why did Ted get your pizza? Why can't I have part of—"

Maureen stood. "Well, kids. I think we've squeezed all the merriment we can out of this day. Let's go home, huh?"

"I wish we could go home to Ohio," said Ted.

"I wish Momma was alive," Kevin said softly.

"I wish I were fifty thousand miles away," said Maureen. "I wish I were on the moon, with no way to get back."

"The moon's more than fifty thousand miles away," Ted said. "It's more like—"

"Oh, for heaven's sake, let's go home," Maureen snapped, walking away.

Looking at them, listening to them, Josh wondered if it ever made sense to envy anyone. When he'd first met the Arthurs they'd seemed so carefree, so happy-go-lucky, not bothering about food or furniture or what lay ahead, just living in a sort of ramshackle day-to-day way, accepting things and people as they came.

He hadn't had a clue, when he first met them, that people who lived like that could ever be unhappy about anything.

12

Cleo came to live at Tincture of Spain when she was three weeks old. Josh decided he had never seen anything else in his life so marvelous as that little wild spotted creature with her silky fur and great padding paws and green eyes. She was as small as a house cat but fifty times stronger, and in one swipe at an armchair demonstrated just how the Arthur furniture had come to be what it had come to be.

Sometimes during her daytime naps, of which she took many, she slept in the crib at the far end of the living room. Ted said the crib had been all of theirs in turn and had been handed over to the animals when Nora outgrew it.

"Cobina and Serena used it last," Ted said.

"I can see their tooth and claw marks on it."

"Oh, those could be Nora's," said Ted, then looked around quickly to be sure his sister wasn't within hearing.

Cleo still had to be fed from a bottle—a baby formula of milk and cereal and vitamins—every four hours, and all the children took turns at this, except Nora, who couldn't hold her. She had sharp little claws and sharp little teeth and a habit of leaping at anything that moved, so that in a few days they were all pitted with small bite marks and shallow scratches.

Dr. Arthur said she hadn't a vicious cell in her system. "Quite unlike her mother," he told them.

"Did Fatima mind having her baby taken away?" Josh asked him.

"She looks rather mournful and prowls more than usual. But her temper hasn't changed. No better and no worse. Not that it could get much worse."

Cleo's mother was one of the few cats that the attendants, including Clara, who didn't seem to be afraid of any animal, refused to enter a cage with. Even the big female tiger lolled at one end of her cage when a favored attendant—Clara, or a man named Frenchy—arrived with bucket, hose, and stiff-bristled broom for the weekly clean-up. Fatima was closed away in the inside cage while the outside one was being done and then outside while the inside one was done.

It made Josh sad to think of her, so mostly he did not, having concluded that the best way not to worry about something was to pretend it didn't exist, wasn't there, hadn't happened.

He'd tried to explain this philosophy to his father once, that time his bike had been smashed up because he'd parked it in a place where a car was practically bound to run into it and a car had. He'd pushed the bike home and shoved it in a corner of the shed. It'd been a couple of weeks before his parents noticed he wasn't riding it, but then one day his mother asked why he'd taken to walking where he used to ride.

"Is it some program of physical fitness?" she'd inquired, sort of idly.

Josh waited a fraction too long before agreeing that yes, he'd decided walking was good exercise.

"Now just a moment," Mr. Redmond had said, coming out from behind his newspaper. "Something's fishy."

"What's fishy, Dad? You're all the time telling me I should walk more, and now I'm walking more."

"You are walking, Josh, all the time. Now that I think of it, I haven't even seen your bicycle for—how long? What's the matter with it?"

"With my bike?"

"Yes, Joshua. With your bike."

"Oh—well, this car ran over it and—"

"When did a car run over it?" his mother said sharply. "How? Josh, were you hurt? What's this all *about*?"

"I'm trying to tell you, Mom. This car—I mean, no I wasn't hurt, I wasn't on it. It was parked, see. Just parked, like always, and this car just ran over it. Or maybe a truck, except it couldn't have been a truck because it'd be in worse shape than it is, unless it was a small truck, like a pick-up, maybe—"

"Josh," said Mr. Redmond. "Get on with it."

"Yeah. Well, probably it was a car, only I wasn't there so I didn't see, and the people who did it just drove off, like Dad says women do in parking lots—back into other people's fenders and lights and things and drive off not leaving a note or anything—"

Mrs. Redmond looked at her husband. "You think it's only women who do that?"

"Don't you know a diversionary tactic when you hear it? I said people do it."

Josh was pretty sure his father had said women, but on occasion was wise enough to hold his tongue. This was such an occasion. But it hadn't been a diversionary tactic, because he knew there wasn't a chance of diverting them onto the subject of careless car parkers in parking lots. They'd narrow in on careless bike parkers.

They got the whole story out of him—where he'd parked his bicycle, just how dumb and thoughtless it had been to put it there.

"Not," said Mr. Redmond, "that that justifies this—person hitting a kid's bicycle and going off without a word. The basic dishonesty of people constantly surprises me, although why, at my age, I should continue to be surprised is a puzzle. Crooks and crackpots abound. What's so surprising about that?"

148

"Josh," said Mrs. Redmond. "How badly banged up is the bicycle?"

"Oh, it's pretty bad," he admitted, since they could, and would, go out to the shed and see for themselves. "Like totaled."

"What I don't see is why you put it in some obscure corner of the shed and just said nothing," his father went on. "Did you think we'd never notice? Or that it would somehow repair itself if you said nothing? I have trouble following your mental processes."

Boy, do you, thought Josh. But he had difficulty in this line himself. Following his own mental processes, or anybody else's. Sometimes he felt that old Mr. Arthur made as good sense being *out* of his senses as other people made who were supposed to be *in* theirs.

"Well," he said to his father, frowning in an effort to find words for what was really not a thought at all, just a feeling. "Well, I guess in a way I did sort of think that."

"Think what?"

"That you'd forget about it, or that somehow—I dunno how exactly, but *somehow*—the bike'd sort of—piece itself together, you know? I mean, I didn't really think that, because that'd be pretty dumb. I just sort of *felt* that if I left it alone and didn't say anything or think about it, it'd all be back the way it used to be. Or I'd be grown up by the time I had to do anything about it. Or think about it."

"Incredible," said Mr. Redmond.

149

"I hope you aren't too mad, Dad?"

"No, just enough."

He'd walked everywhere from then till the following Christmas, when they'd gotten him a new bicycle and, all things considered, hadn't offered him too much advice about how to take care of it.

All the same, Josh continued to be of the opinion that the best way to deal with something worrisome was not to worry about it. So he put Cleo's mother and her miserable life, about which he could do nothing, out of his mind, and concentrated on having fun with Cleo.

"But what'll happen to her," he asked Dr. Arthur, "when she gets big? If she's very gentle, can you keep her forever?"

"Out of the question. These cats outgrow domestic life, and we have to come to terms with that from the day we take them. With Cobina and Serena we got so attached to them that it was a terrible wrench when they had to go to the zoo."

"Cobina and Serena live mainly on farina," said old Mr. Arthur.

The three of them were sitting on the terrace where Josh, to his surprise, had found Dr. Arthur sitting with his father this late in the morning. It was nine thirty. By Dr. Arthur's standards the middle of the day. When Josh had asked where the kids were, Dr. Arthur had looked around, as if surprised to find them still gone, and said, "Oh, they went out a while ago. Should be back pretty soon. In fact, they have to be. I can't leave Pop alone."

Josh thought of offering to stay with the old man himself, but then did not. He wasn't sure that Mr. Arthur would stay with him, or that he'd be able to calm him if the old man got upset.

Cleo was sound asleep in her crib, clutching a Raggedy Ann doll. Josh had stood and looked down at her and then come out here on the terrace with the two Arthur men and asked about Cleo's future.

"Cobina and Serena live mainly on farina," old Mr. Arthur said again, very loudly, then suddenly twisted in his chair and got to his feet. "Let me out of here," he said, his old face bright with panic. "Let me out, I tell you!"

"Pop," said Dr. Arthur, putting a calming hand on his father's arm. "Pop, sit down again. Everything's all right."

"Oh, it is, is it?"

"Yes, everything's just fine."

"If you say so," Mr. Arthur said, sitting tentatively on the edge of his chair. He sounded unconvinced.

"No, really Pop. It's fine, just fine."

"I see." He relaxed and leaned back, and Dr. Arthur looked at him a moment before turning back to Josh. "The time comes when the cats, or the aardvarks, or—" He looked at his father again "—whatever—have to be put away, locked up, because they're unfit to live on

151

their own. Anyway, where would they live? The animals, I mean. There's not enough wilderness left to support them."

"There must be some, like in South America or Africa," Josh ventured.

"In Africa and South America, despite laws against it, the killing of animals for their hides or their tusks or just for the joy of killing—and you'll never eliminate the joy of killing from the human breast—continues at a rate that guarantees the annihilation of all but the hardiest species. And then you have the incursion of man with his agricultural needs, his industrial greed, using up land at such a rate that even if the animals were not being shot and trapped in such wholesale fashion, they'll eventually disappear because they'll have no place to live, no place to hide. Of course, we're going to bring ourselves and everything else down with us, which is a comfort, I suppose."

"A comfort?"

"I like the idea of our evening up our destruction of the planet by destroying ourselves along with it. It appeals to my sense of justice."

"But that'd mean we'd all be dead."

"Yup," said Dr. Arthur.

Overwhelmed, Josh could do nothing but stare at this man who talked in such a gentle voice and said such frightening things. Even his father, who thought a lot of the same things that Dr. Arthur did, never came right out and said them so flatly. His father always hedged a little, giving the world just an outside chance.

"Man and nature," Dr. Arthur went on, "have never been able to live in harmony. But during the ascendency of nature, which lasted millions, billions of years, what change there was—the elimination of species, the shiftings of land and water masses—was the gradual product of natural forces. No cruelty, no gluttony, no *sport*."

"Nature can be cruel," said Josh. "There's this little blue heron that used to hang around Powers' Bait and Tackle Shop. He was there for years, and Clooney and his dad would throw him dead shrimp from the bait tank, and if they accidentally left it open he'd help himself. A little thief, they called him, but they liked him. Everybody did. And then one day he showed up with a big chip off his beak, and he couldn't catch the shrimp they tried to give him. The shrimp just dropped into the water every time he tried to catch it. Mr. Powers tried to catch him, maybe take him to the vet and see if he could be patched up, but he flew away and they never saw him again. Mr. Powers said he'd die of starvation, and he said that chip came probably from being hit by some bigger bird, or maybe it was snapped off by a crab or something. I mean, Mr. Powers said no person could've done it. So that was nature, wasn't it? And cruel."

Dr. Arthur didn't agree. "Nature is harsh, inexorable. But without malice."

Josh stirred unhappily, wishing the others would

153

come back or that he felt easy enough with Dr. Arthur just to get up and leave. He was never really comfortable with Ted's father, who made him think about things he didn't want to think about, who practically never laughed, who was very kind to his father and children when he was with them, but just about never was.

"Only man," Dr. Arthur mused, "is deliberately cruel, because only man knows what cruelty is."

Oh boy, thought Josh. Oh golly. And to think that he'd wanted to get his father and Dr. Arthur together because they had sort of the same ideas about things. One of them was bad enough. With both of them explaining how rotten mankind was and how the world was going to be polished off any minute, a guy got so he hardly thought it was worthwhile growing up.

He'd said that to his father one day. He'd said, "If the world's going to be blown up, like you say—"

"As I say. Not that I quite—"

"As, as, as," Josh had interrupted. "If it's going to be blown up or dried up or used up like—as—you say, then why should I bother going to school? What's the point in learning a lot of stuff I won't be around to know?"

"I didn't say the world was going to end tomorrow, Joshua. I'm not even guaranteeing its demise—"

"Gee, you're not?"

"I'm not," his father had said calmly, ignoring the sneer in Josh's voice. "I don't hold out much hope for it. For us. Which doesn't mean that I'm altogether without hope. But even if I were, that is no reason to throw up our hands and say there's no use to anything. We must always remember Martin Luther, who said, 'Even if I knew the world would end tomorrow, I'd still plant my apple tree.' A healthy philosophy we would all do well to follow."

Josh had thought, but not said, that to him Martin Luther sounded nuts and if he, Josh, personally knew the world would end tomorrow, he'd—well, what? He didn't know. Yell, probably.

"If you knew the world would end tomorrow," he said now to Dr. Arthur, "what would you do?"

Dr. Arthur looked at him the way Mr. Greene once in a while had, when he'd showed some promise of understanding what the lesson was about. "That's an interesting thing for you to ask," Dr. Arthur said. "Did you ever hear of the great German religious reformer, Martin Luther?"

"Yup. He planted apple trees. Or said he would." At Dr. Arthur's expression of surprise, Josh added, "My father—he talks about the end of the world, too, and then tells me what Martin Luther would've done about it." Apparently everyone who was looking for the world to end knew that Martin Luther would have planted a tree. "I was just wondering what you would do. Or my father. I only seem to find out what Martin Luther would've done."

He jumped as a furry body hurled itself at his leg.

Front paws gripping his knee and pulling it toward her, Cleo worked with her hind legs to push his ankle away. With a rush of joy, Josh forgot about Dr. Arthur, Martin Luther, his father, and the end of the world.

"I never even heard her coming, did you?" he asked, leaning over to pick up the sturdy, squirming, silky little animal with the surprisingly strong muscles and deep growl. She struggled in his arms for a moment, clutching his hand in her mouth, then all at once settled down with her broad head resting trustfully on his knees and began to purr. Josh remained immobile, not wanting by the slightest movement to make her feel unwelcome. He took deep slow breaths and was happy, absolutely happy. He was still sitting there, stiffening but resolute, his joy in her not one drop diminished, when Ted and Maureen came in, followed by Kevin and Nora. They had the baby carriage loaded with grocery bags.

"Oh, that's where you were," Dr. Arthur said. "Josh here was wondering. So was I."

"I told you before we left, Dad," said Maureen. "I said we were going to get the marketing done for a whole week."

"You did? Well, I have to get along. Take care of Pop."

Mr. Arthur struggled out of his chair with some difficulty—it was a gray day, the kind when his arthritis seemed to gnaw at his bones—and attempted to follow his son. "I'll be going along with this fellow," he said to

Ted, apparently feeling the need to explain his actions to somebody. "I'll just go with him." He put a gnarled hand toward Dr. Arthur, who closed his eyes, then opened them again with an expression of pain.

"Pop," he said, "you can't. You can't come with me."

"That's right," said the old man. "That's what I said, all right. With you. I'm going with you—" He was still holding his hand out, and Maureen dumped a bag of groceries on the table, spilling out cans and bottles, and went to take her grandfather's hand in both of hers.

"Now now, Granddad darling," she coaxed. "Some other time. You stay with Ted and me, now, okay?"

"And with us," said Kevin. "You stay with all of us, Granddad. I'll play checkers with you, okay?"

At first Mr. Arthur seemed not to hear them, but in a moment he nodded. "I see. All right. I'll stay here." He turned his back to his son and walked unsteadily to his chair on the terrace where he spent so much of his time. Josh, thinking back to that first day he'd seen Mr. Arthur, realized with surprise how much—older, and sort of frailer, sicker, he seemed now than he had seemed then. And it wasn't all that long ago, either.

He wondered, and wondered why he hadn't thought of it before, and why the Arthurs didn't seem to be thinking of it, what was going to happen when school opened. Who'd take care of Mr. Arthur then? He wasn't safe left alone. Somebody had to be on the watch all the time, to see that he didn't wander out into the road, or

157

burn himself on the stove, or do any of the things that a very old man, or a very little kid, might do if left on his own.

Dr. Arthur still hadn't left. He was standing in the doorway, staring at his father with that expression of terrible sadness in his eyes. Finally he sighed and said he'd have to be going.

"Take care of him," he said again. He turned his head slowly from side to side and added, "Old age, let me tell you, is not for sissies."

He was gone.

13

"Old age is not for sissies, that's what he said," Josh told his parents that afternoon. "It seemed sad, you know."

Mrs. Redmond said she did know. Her duties at the Shelter Workshop took her into association with the terrible sadness of old age. But at least, she said, Mr. Arthur had a family who loved him. "Many of the aged have also to face total loneliness."

"What I don't quite see," said Mr. Redmond, "is what's to be done about the old man."

"When school starts, you mean," said Josh, and his father nodded. Some day he thought he'd tell his father how funny it was that often he'd be thinking something and his father would say it, or answer it. Some day he'd tell him. Not right now.

"Maybe they can afford a nurse or something, during school hours," Mrs. Redmond said.

159

"I don't think so," Josh said slowly. "They seem awfully poor to me. I mean, that's why Dr. Beldon left the zoo, wasn't it, because he couldn't afford to take care of his family on what they paid him; and he didn't have as big a family as Dr. Arthur."

"Then what will they do? They appear to be really improvident. Don't seem to think ahead at all."

"How do you know they aren't thinking ahead?" Josh said heatedly. "How do we know what they're thinking?"

"I thought you might know. They've taken you in as one of the family. At least, it seems that way."

"Well, they have, I guess. But people in families don't always tell other people in it what they're thinking, do they?"

"Now, Joshua," said his father, who often said *Now, Joshua*, meaning he didn't intend to give an answer at the moment, if ever. "None of our business, anyway."

"I don't know about that," Mrs. Redmond began, and Josh said with alarm, "Mother, it *isn't*. Our business. They aren't delinquents or something that you can boss around—"

"Joshua, I resent that. I do not boss people around. My entire purpose in the work I do is to help people, and I am experienced in helping people who can't help themselves."

"Yeah, Mom, I know. I'm sorry. I take it back. Only, please don't help the Arthurs, huh? They can take care of themselves, and like Dad says, I mean as Dad says, it's none of our business."

"You mean you don't care how they solve their problems?"

"Mom, I mean I only want to be friends with them. How would you like it if some friend of mine's mother came snooping around here telling you and Dad to—to like get the dock fixed up because it's dangerous this way. I mean, it is, and we all know it is and nobody does anything about it, but if some friend of mine's mother came snoo—"

"All right, Josh," said Mr. Redmond. "We get your point."

"You get it, maybe," said Josh, not satisfied. "It's if Mom gets it, that's what I'm—"

"You can stop worrying," his mother said coldly. "I shall not attempt to help your friends in any way."

"Aw gee," said Josh, wondering why it was he and his parents got these bad vibes so much. If they ever even *noticed* anything, it'd help. Like it had been weeks since he'd lost his temper, but had anybody said to him, "Josh, how come you don't lose your temper anymore?" or, "Son, we notice you don't lose your temper anymore and that's very good, we congratulate you."

But no, not a word. For all they observed, he might as well still be pitching four-minute eggs at the kitchen wall. A thing he'd done only once, of course. You didn't do that twice. Not in the Redmond kitchen.

161

If they had asked him, he might have explained (or he might not have) that a couple of months of watching Nora throw herself on the floor and bellow, and even— as he had used to do himself—bang her forehead against things, had about convinced him that losing your temper that way might be okay for kids four years old, but probably was something a person ought to outgrow. Even before he'd met the Arthurs he'd begun to get tired of losing control of himself. It had got to be a nuisance, and he was glad to be past it, and he figured he really was pretty much past it. It was like getting—the mumps, for instance—behind you. Mumps and temper tantrums were just things it was better to have already had.

Come to think of it, his parents hadn't congratulated him on getting over the mumps, either. Nobody had said, "Son, we are heartily pleased to see that you have faced up to the difficulty of having mumps and have safely put them behind you. You are to be congratulated."

Maybe they didn't think about it at all, except to feel he'd had mumps rather early and tantrums pretty late in his life. Probably they'd just assumed all along that he'd get over his bursts of rage, because it was the only sensible thing to do, and they expected him, as they often said, to be sensible.

Which was more than Hank Burroughs' mother and father expected Hank to be.

"What are you smiling at, Josh?" his mother asked.

"I was just thinking—" He looked at them, trans-

162

ferred his gaze to the ceiling. "I was just thinking that you two are pretty good parents."

There was a short silence and then Mr. Redmond said, "That's a nice thing to say, Joshua. Very nice. We think you're a pretty good son."

Mrs. Redmond didn't say anything. She cleared her throat a little, and as she got up to take the dishes from the table, ran a hand over Josh's head.

Going out on the dock with scraps, Josh was still smiling contentedly. A laughing gull, perched on one of the lanterns, threw his head back, opened his scarlet mouth, and cackled shrilly.

"Okay, okay, I'm coming," said Josh, and in seconds the air above his head was swirling with gulls and terns, who at first insisted he toss the bits of bread and meat to them, where they easily hawked them on the wing, but in a little while took to swooping past and picking scraps from his fingers. They were delicate and precise, and never in the years that he'd been feeding them had Josh felt a nip from one of those curved beaks.

When the food was gone the birds scattered, shrieking. Two pelicans, gravely riding the waters near the dock, remained for a while, hopeful of a handout, but they were no match for the gulls and Josh had never yet been able to feed both species at the same time. He resorted to trickery to feed the pelicans, luring them onto the dock with fish heads, which he practically had to shield with his body against the gulls. Once the pelicans

163

brought themselves to come up on the dock, Josh could feed them by hand, but each time he had to make his peaceable, his bountiful intentions plain all over again. He did not think pelicans were awfully bright, not nearly as alert, or as beautiful, as gulls or terns. Or skimmers, with their narrow, arrowy bodies. In fact, when you came right down to it, and right close to them, pelicans were pretty homely, while the trees and the sky around Lands End just swarmed with birds that really were downright beautiful. So why he went on preferring pelicans to any others he didn't know.

He looked down now at these two angular big fellows who floated with their eyes fixed on his face. "Sorry, guys," he said. "I don't have time to win you over just now. Don't have any fish heads, come to that. Besides, you know as well as I do that those fellows—" he gestured toward some distant gulls who flew apparently oblivious of the dock, the boy, and the pelicans "—would be here in a snap if I did bring anything out for you."

The pelicans bobbed a moment longer and then came about and headed away.

And I said they weren't bright, Josh thought to himself, sauntering back down the dock and going into the living room, where his father was at his desk, going over some books.

"We could go clamming, Dad. Mom could make fritters and chowder." His mouth watered as he thought of his mother's fritters and chowder.

Mr. Redmond hesitated, and Josh waited for him to say he was too busy. "Have to work on these ledgers," he'd say probably. Oh well, he'd go clamming by himself. Or he'd go over and see if Ted'd go with him. Then he could teach Maureen how to make clam chowder the way it should be made, although he didn't think he'd quite be up to fritters. If the Arthur kids got into the habit of clamming, they wouldn't have to eat hot dogs so much. Not that Josh had anything against hot dogs, but just the same—

"Okay," said Mr. Redmond. "Let's go."

Josh looked at his father with surprise, then said he'd get the buckets. He thought of asking if he could run over and pick up Ted, but was afraid his father would then say, "Oh well, if you have Ted you don't need me." Today, just now, he thought he'd like best to be with his father, just the two of them.

Out on the flats, other people with the same notion were scooping with hands deep into the sand to bring up quahogs and sunrays. Josh, who'd been clamming for years, got his bucket filled quickly. It was just a matter of looking for the little keyhole-like aperture in the sand, then quickly shoving both hands deep enough to snare the clam. Quahogs were rough and gray-shelled, sunrays polished and beautiful with a design on each side that looked as if a rising sun had been painted there.

Mr. Redmond, who'd also been clamming since childhood, kept forgetting what he was there for. He stared about, breathing the hot brine-filled air with evident pleasure, smiling faintly, almost in the way he did at the tiller on *Candide*. He pointed out to Josh a flock of white ibises perambulating past in shallow water, thrusting in unison their long curved red beaks into the waves, then lifting their heads to stare about imperiously before marching on. He dug a clam or two, and then drew Josh's attention to a boat out on the Gulf.

"Beautiful rig," he said. "What kind is it, Josh?"

Josh straightened, studied the boat. Fore and aft masts. Foremast shorter. Jib and foresail set. "Schooner?"

"Yup. Don't see that kind of rig much anymore."

"Why not?"

"Oh, not fast enough, I guess. But isn't she a honey? Look, they're putting up the main. Look at that, will you?"

Josh and his father stared after the boat as, full-rigged on a broad reach, she headed away from them out to sea.

An elderly man, his bucket full, stopped to greet them. Mr. Wise, a customer of his father's.

"How was the race, Pete?" said Mr. Redmond.

"Oh, great, great. Heavy weather all the way. We tacked all the way down, and then the wind changed just as we rounded the buoy at Boca Grande, so we tacked all the way back." He laughed. "Came in just ahead of the class behind us."

"Whose boat were you on?"

"Forester's, from Miami. A fifty-foot cutter."

"*Calendula?*"

166

"That's the one. The crew was mostly kids, like your-self—" Mr. Wise stopped and smiled at Josh. "All things are relative. To me, your father's a kid."

Josh stared at his father, and both men laughed heart-ily at his expression. "I was trying to tell these other—kids," said Mr. Wise, "that they don't know how easy things are for them these days—Dacron sails, aluminum masts, fiber glass hulls—"

"We have a mahogany hull on *Candide*," said Josh.

"Oh, I know that, young fellow. Your father's an old-timey sailor despite his tender years. But he uses Dacron sails, all right."

"Don't tell me you're still using cotton?" asked Mr. Redmond with a smile.

Mr. Wise admitted that he did not. "But I think about the old days sometimes, when a boat was *work*. They're just toys now, nothing but toys. Well, home to the chowder maker. See you."

Josh looked after him, but his father's attention had now been caught by a pair of porpoises plunging past in languid curves, their sleek bodies gleaming like pew-ter.

By the time Mr. Redmond had his bucket full, most of the other clammers had left and the tide was rising. Going out to the flats from Lands End they'd walked on wet sand. Coming back, they were knee-deep in water.

They washed the clams on the dock, and then in the

167

kitchen Mr. Redmond, with a heavy knife, opened them, tossing the meat into a large wooden bowl for chopping, which Josh did. Mrs. Redmond was prepared to make fritters and chowder if, she always told them, they did all the real work. Chopping away, Josh thought that there were times when real work was all fun. He wondered why it was that once in a while his parents, especially his father, could be so great to be with while other times the three of them were as testy with each other as —as a flock of seagulls.

As his father couldn't open clams as fast as Josh could chop them, he leaned on his elbows, thinking. It was all sort of hard to understand. Maybe there wasn't any answer, any way of understanding. Maybe the answer was just that that's how people are, which was no answer at all, so in the end there was no point in thinking about it at all. Just enjoy a day like today and hope there'd be another, not too far off.

He resumed chopping. His father reached across him and flicked on a wall switch, and the lanterns at the end of the dock went on in the fading light.

"You know," Mr. Redmond said suddenly, "I sort of miss it."

"Miss what?"

"That constant talk of yours. Used to drive me crazy, just about, and now I find I miss it. There's no pleasing human beings, is there?"

"Don't I talk as much as I used to?"

"This summer seems to have slowed you down appre-

168

ciably. We were thinking maybe it was having to talk in competition with all the young Arthurs and the old man."

"Maybe it was. Is." Josh chopped a minute, and said, "I didn't notice that. That I wasn't talking much—"

"I didn't say you weren't talking much. I said you weren't talking all the time."

"I didn't notice," Josh said again. "I mean, I *know* I don't lose my temper anymore—" He glanced up at his father's face.

Mr. Redmond nodded. "We'd observed that, too. And in no way do I miss that."

"Well, but that I did on purpose. Stopped, I mean. Losing it. I decided it was—kiddish."

"So it is. You're to be congratulated."

Josh started slightly, then grinned. "Oh, no. It's like getting over the mumps."

"I assure you, it is not," Mr. Redmond said seriously. "There are people who continue at the mercy of their own intemperate tempers their entire lives, which puts other people at their mercy, too. There are few qualities harder on everyone around than an undisciplined disposition, and a person who works on bringing his under control is to be highly complimented."

"Well gee. Thanks."

"Don't mention it. There are too many clams here for the three of us. Why don't you take some over to the Arthurs?"

"That'd be great. Tell you what, Dad. I'll take some

to them and tell Ted and Maureen how to make a chowder, and then I'll be right back. You tell Mom to start on the fritters right away, okay? Tell her we're starving."

"That's no lie," said Mr. Redmond, as Josh went out the door whistling.

14

Toward the end of August a hurricane in the Caribbean caused the residents of Florida and the Gulf coast states to pay more than customary attention to weather reports.

"You got your chart up?" Ted asked Josh.

"What chart?"

"Your storm-plotting chart. My father got ours yesterday." He pointed proudly to a large map Scotch-taped to the kitchen door. It showed the Gulf of Mexico, part of Mexico itself, the Caribbean with Haiti and the Dominican Republic, the Straits of Florida, and the Atlantic Ocean up to Cape Hatteras. It was clearly marked with latitudinal and longitudinal lines.

"We don't use one, actually," said Josh.

"You don't?" said Ted, in a tone of disappointment.

"Then how do you plot the course of the storm? I've got these pins ready, to plot it, after you show me how."

"I don't think I can. I mean, like I say, we don't have one." He looked at the chart. "I guess you just listen to the broadcasts and stick in pins."

"You're some help. Well, anyway, tell me the terminology. What's it called, what we're in now? A hurricane alert? A hurricane watch?"

"It isn't called anything yet. We aren't in one."

"When it *is*, when we are. What do you say then?"

"We usually just say a storm is coming."

"What's the matter with you, Josh?"

"I dunno."

What was the matter with him? He felt sort of glum. He thought it had something to do with his father, and how every time he was friendly and great to be with for a while, maybe even a week or so, then he closed up like a quahog again and didn't listen or talk.

"I'll tell you one thing," he said, "if I ever have a kid—I'm not going to have one, I'm not going to get married or anything—but if I accidentally should have one, then I'm gonna talk to him, and listen to him. All the time, I mean. Not just on-again, off-again."

Ted, who was now wrestling on the floor with a Cleo twice the size she'd been on the day she first arrived, said, "I don't get it. Why're you always worrying about what your father does, for Pete's sake?"

"I'm not always worrying, I—"

172

"Why are you ever worrying, is what I mean. I mean, if you come right down to it, what's it got to do with you?"

"What's it got to do with *me*? I live with him, he's my father, that's what it's got to do with me."

"I live with mine too, and I never know what he's up to, except, you know, the things he does every day, like eat and go to work. Don't get me wrong, I want him to be okay and all, but that's his problem, isn't it? I got enough to do figuring how to keep myself together, without worrying about my father and if he is or isn't talking to me, which come to think of it, most of the time he isn't, like yours."

Cleo bounded away from Ted and hurled herself at Josh, who dropped to the floor and began to bat her gently about. She sprang at his bare arm, grasping his wrist in her teeth, not so gently. Not, he told himself, trying unsuccessfully to push her away, that she meant to be as strong as she was. She just was.

"That's okay for you, I guess," he said, holding the wriggling cat close to his chest, enjoying the deep sound of her growl, which as yet was purely playful. "You've got Maureen and Kev and even Nora to talk with. To be with. I guess I just don't like being an only. Maybe that's all that's wrong."

"Why don't you ask your Mommy and Daddy to give you a baby brother?"

"I'll throw this cat at you, that's what I'll do."

Ted laughed. "You can have one of my sisters or

my brother. You can have them all. I'll keep Cleo and you take the rest of them. Find out what it's like *not* to be an only. Trouble with you is you don't know when you're well off. Did I tell you Cleo sleeps with me now?"

"She *does*?"

"Yeah. Right at my feet. That's why they're so bruised and bloody. She likes me to stay still and once in a while I move around." He cuffed Cleo lovingly. "Some bunkmate you are," he told her.

Pedaling home, observing the strange stillness that seemed to lie over sea and shore, noting how the evening birds did not seem to be singing, or even to be around, Josh wondered if what was wrong with him was, after all, just something to do with the weather.

Maybe a hurricane was coming their way, at that. Usually before a storm there was this peculiar kind of predicting calm in the atmosphere. The air quiet, the sea flat as a dish of jello. Out on Catfish Island he could see in the gathering dusk what appeared to be hundreds more than the usual number of sea birds clustered on the shore. Those birds that were flying flew low.

"If a hurricane is going to come," Ted had asked, getting back to the subject, "where will it hit?"

"Can't tell yet. That's what your chart is for," Josh had added with a little grin. "You'll be the first to know, so give me a high sign when you find out, okay?"

"Sure. How long does it take for a hurricane to hit us, after it gets started in the Caribbean, I mean?"

174

"Couple of days, maybe. Depends on how fast it's traveling. You sound like you want us to be hit."

"Be sort of exciting, wouldn't it?"

Josh had to agree that it could be that. "I've only been in one real one. The rest always hit above or below us, and that's still plenty of excitement, believe me. After that real one, that was years ago, Clooney Powers and I rowed a boat right down the streets of the village, getting salvage."

"What sort of salvage?"

"Anything that had floated away from its house that we could get into the boat. Half the houses on the Gulf side had floated away themselves. Well, maybe not half."

"This side? These houses?" Ted whistled.

"There was this house, down about a couple of miles, the whole back of it just dropped into the water, so we could see right into all the rooms."

"Hey, boy," said Ted. "Don't tell Maureen any of this, huh? She's already screaming to go back to Ohio. If she thought the back of the house was going to come loose and flap off, there'd be no living with her. There practically isn't now, since Dad took that Clara out to dinner one night."

Josh wasn't interested in that. He was getting into the hurricane spirit of things, thinking that maybe a coming storm accounted for his lowness of spirit. It took some people that way.

Except, he thought, putting his bike in the garage,

now that he'd worked that out—or had Ted, really, work it out for him—he oddly enough began to feel just the opposite. Sort of buoyant, sort of electric.

"Hey, Mom," he said, bursting through the kitchen door, "remember that time Clooney and I rowed all through the village after the hurricane, getting salvage? Remember I got that neat captain's chair and the teak lid off a bait well and the brass pot?"

Mrs. Redmond, who still kept flowers in the brass pot, nodded and tried, with little success, to smile. The captain's chair was out on the back porch, and they'd made a table out of the teak lid—and it was a pretty little table at that. "A hurricane is a big price to pay for a table, a chair, and a brass pot," she said. "I hope we aren't in for another one. I just—hope we aren't. I'm not sure I could get through another one."

"What would you do instead?" Josh asked curiously.

"Oh, Josh. Nothing instead. You know that. I'd stay here, as we have always stayed through storms. I think I'm just getting to be too old to find them more exciting than awful. I used to love them."

"You aren't getting old," Josh said irritably, but a moment later he was jigging around, that electric sensation coursing through him. "Hey, we better get a ham cooked and start boiling eggs and potatoes and get *Candide* into the bayou. What d'ya think, Mom?"

"I think we'd better just pay attention to the broadcasts. Have you heard anything lately?"

176

"No, but Ted's got a storm-plotting chart and a bunch of colored pins and he's going to keep us informed."

She did smile then, but only a little. "All right. Between Ted and the U.S. Weather Bureau I guess we'll know when to start laying in stores."

On Friday, Mr. Redmond arrived home early. "Just to be on the safe side, we stowed everything away at the shop. Not a nail left outside. Josh, I think we'd better get *Candide* into the bayou."

"I think we should too," said Josh, remembering the time they'd put off moving her into the relatively quiet waters of the bayou until it was almost too late. They'd had to wrestle her in when the storm had already sent the seas into tumbled disorder, with waves seeming to pile every which way.

He and his father walked down the dock, jumped into the skiff, and motored out to *Candide*, afloat at her mooring. Mr. Redmond fastened a line to her bow, sent Josh to take the tiller, and then with no sense of hurry towed her over the gently lifting and falling waters, through the inlet into the bayou, where he anchored her alongside the seawall.

They ran the skiff back but did not secure it in the usual place. Mr. Redmond detached the engine and lifted it to the dock. It was heavy, but Mr. Redmond, bracing himself in the swaying boat, hoisted it easily. Josh's father had biceps like rocks and the balance of a

177

sailor. It made him, thought Josh, pleasant to watch at work.

"Think it's going to be a real storm?" Josh asked as his father rowed toward the beach.

"Can't guess. Come on, Josh." They stepped into shallow water and pulled the skiff up and far back on the sand.

"We'll get *Scorch* and the canoe well back," said Mr. Redmond, "but let's leave the motor on the dock. No point battening down too much before we find out if we have to batten at all. Let's get some dry clothes on."

A couple of hours later, with the waters restless and rising, radio announcements indicated that while the brunt of the storm was probably going to hit nearly seventy miles away, no one, and certainly not the U.S. Weather Bureau, would be so rash as to make positive predictions where a tropical storm was concerned. Battening was going to be necessary. Gale winds and high seas were certain. Evacuation might, in certain areas be—

"Well," said Mr. Redmond, "let's get at it."

Which means, Josh thought, that he's given up relying on weather reports and is just going on his own instinct. Which, so far as Josh was concerned, meant the storm was on its way.

And now he became aware of the strange sort of sighing wind that came before a storm. It troubled the trees, troubled the air, troubled, in some eerie way, the mind.

"Come on, Josh," said Mr. Redmond.

Getting at it involved moving everything from the back porch around the house to a shed built well back in the trees for this purpose. All the nets, life preservers, oars, paddles, *Scorch*'s mast and centerboard, the deck chairs, Josh's basket of shells collected but not yet sorted, Mrs. Redmond's potted plants, the engine, and the redwood chairs from the dock. While Josh and his father went back and forth, arms laden, Mrs. Redmond cooked food they could eat cold in case the power failed, checked their store of candles and of kerosene for the lamps, filled both bathtubs and all the sinks with water, and stacked piles of old towels underneath each window and along the doorsills, ready to be wedged in if the storm got bad enough.

All the while the sky was darkening to a mustardy gray. The bay waters were now heaping and swelling and riding toward shore in leaden combers. The sighing wind shook and flung the branches of Australian pines, tossed long palm fronds so that they stretched inland, rustled angrily in bushes. It moaned around the house, hurled pieces of driftwood through the darkening air. Although it was not nearly time yet for high tide, the water along the jetty had already reached the normal high tide line.

Josh, going indoors with his father when they'd stowed or chained down, it seemed to him, everything but the trees themselves, wondered how the Arthurs were faring with their preparations. He wondered if they'd even made any, beyond pinning up the hurricane chart. He didn't think they'd ever been faced with an advancing storm that might just turn into a hurricane, and the chart wasn't going to help them much even if Ted got the pins in the right places.

"You know—" he began, as his father said, "I think, Josh—"

They stopped, eyed each other, and waited.

"You first," said Mr. Redmond.

"I was wondering what Ted and the others were doing. I mean, I'm not sure they'll think about things like candles and water and stuff. And they never have any food ahead. I thought I'd better phone and—"

"I think," said Mr. Redmond, "that we'd better get them over here. Just in case."

"Here?" Josh looked from his father to his mother. "They might have to stay, once they got here."

"That's what your father means," said Mrs. Redmond. "If we leave them over there in that hulk—or are they evacuating that side of the island?"

"Hasn't been anything about it on the radio," said Mr. Redmond. "Perhaps they don't think it's necessary."

"Well, by the time they decide, those poor people may be terrified. We'd better ask them to come here, Josh."

"But, Mom—I don't think you've got the picture. I mean, I'd like it fine if we did, but they've got—an awful lot of people. That is, a lot more people than we're used to in this house. And there's Cleo, you know. And you've never met old Mr. Arthur. He can be kind of a problem—"

"Are you trying to say you don't want us to have them here, Josh?" Mrs. Redmond said sharply.

"No, I'm not," he snapped. "I'm trying to say I don't think you do. Not really."

"Let us be the judge of that, all right?" Mrs. Redmond said, adding, "Sorry, Josh. There's something about storms that makes people hasty. Electricity, or something. Let's call your friends."

"Better yet," said Mr. Redmond, "let's drive over. Look, dear," he said to his wife, "while Josh and I are on our way over, you telephone Dr. Arthur and tell him what we think—that they'd do better to come over to our side of the island and stay with us, until we see how bad this is going to be. Tell them to lock their windows and doors and—well, you know," he said, turning back to give his wife a light kiss. "Tell them we'll be there in a few minutes."

15

Dr. Arthur had taken the van and gone to the zoo, to see to the animals.

"The animals," said Mr. Redmond. "Well, yes. Of course." He could see, he said, that the animals would have to be attended to. He looked around the vast living room, where a couple of floor lamps seemed to cast shadow more than give light. Vaulted ceiling and corners receded into darkness. More than ever, Josh thought, it gave an underground cave effect.

"What the devil?" said Mr. Redmond, looking down.

"That's just Cleo, sir," said Ted, picking up a wildly unconsenting jaguar whose eyes glittered as she bared her teeth and uttered her full deep growl. "Just greeting you," Ted assured him.

"Mmm," said Mr. Redmond, smiling at Ted, the only one of Arthur children he'd already met. Josh introduced Maureen and Kevin, who said how do you do, and Nora, who narrowed her eyes and said nothing. "Come on over here and meet Mr. Arthur, Dad," said Josh, pulling his father toward the sliding glass doors, tightly closed now. Mr. Arthur was sitting in his chair in front of them, apparently dumbfounded by the sight of the Gulf. No wonder, thought Josh. The waters of the bay were calm in comparison to these surging seas that ran at the shore, seeming hardly, in their forward rush, to recede at all. They crashed toward the beach, lifting in great walls that seemed to hang and hesitate before crashing downward, foaming and furious.

"Granddad," said Josh, "here's my father." He caught a look of surprise on his father's face. "I just got in the habit. He knows who Granddad is, but Mr. Arthur doesn't mean anything to him."

Mr. Arthur struggled to his feet, put out his right hand and swept off his beret with the left. "There you are," he said. "There you are and here I am, and what do you make of that?"

"Well, I—"

"If it's all same to you," Mr. Arthur went on, "there's three of them here, or maybe four, but whatever you say, whatever you say—not much time in any case, eh, not much time at all—two or five, makes no difference —not much time, though—"

"Actually there isn't," Mr. Redmond began, and then stared at Josh and the other children. He turned back to Mr. Arthur and said, "Not much time, you're right. We'll just get everything set and get on with it."

"That's right, that's right," said Mr. Arthur. "There's five. Now those out there—" he gestured at the glass doors "—don't know what we'll do about those, all of them out there, going around and around that way—"

"They'll come, too," said Mr. Redmond, and Ted smiled at him.

"Come where?" Maureen asked. She was looking perplexed and a little resentful. "Where are we coming? Going?"

"My parents think it'd be better if you all came over to our house," Josh explained. "I mean, it may still be just a bad blow and everything may be fine here. But just in case."

"In case what?" Maureen insisted.

Mr. Redmond, who'd involuntarily looked up at the beam where Senator Freebee had been found swinging gently, brought his eyes down and said to Maureen, "The houses on the Gulf side, in a really heavy storm, much less a hurricane if it comes close, can be pretty badly hit. So far—except for once many years ago— we've always weathered them okay on the bay side. Power goes and the water has made it over the deck to the living-room doors, but, except for that one

184

time, no worse. Over here—well, you just can't tell."

Maureen seemed doubtful and Josh thought he hardly blamed her. Here his parents had never made a move to meet any of them, and the first time they did it was with the purpose of hauling the entire family out of its house to theirs.

"Really, Maureen," he urged. "It'd be better. Didn't my mother call you?" Maureen shook her head. "That's funny," said Josh. "She was going to, while Dad and I drove over."

Ted went into the kitchen, came back shrugging. "No phone is why. It's dead."

"Look, kids," said Mr. Redmond, "we'll get all your doors and windows closed, and you get some clothes together, enough for a couple of days and nights—"

"We gonna stay at your house?" Kevin asked, and Nora began to wail.

"I won't! I don't wanna! I don't like that man! Maureen, tell that man to go away!"

"Mr. Redmond," Maureen began, "I'm awfully sorry. She—"

"Really, we don't have time for all this," he said. Let's— Josh, you and Ted see to the windows and doors, and if you'll get the children's things, Maureen, and things for your grandfather. Oh, and leave a note for your father. We'll try to telephone him, but if our line is down, too—"

By the time they left, Nora still sobbing protests,

Kevin in a state of barely controlled excitement, Ted holding Cleo who didn't wish to be held, old Mr. Arthur clutching his beret against the wind and asking over and over who all these people were, it was fully dark and the rain was beginning.

As they drove from Tincture of Spain the first huge drops splattered against the windshield of Mr. Redmond's crowded car. By the time they'd made the short drive to the other side of the island water streamed down the glass, making wipers useless. At the house, Josh got out, drenched immediately as if he'd walked into the ocean, and hurled the garage door up so that his father could drive in and the rest of them get out in the dry and lighted garage and make their way in through the kitchen, where Mrs. Redmond stopped cooking to great them as calmly and cordially as if they'd arrived for afternoon tea.

They milled around, the big kitchen seeming all at once quite small.

Old Mr. Arthur said, "If you'll excuse me, please," and started out the door.

Ted grabbed at him, turned him around and said, "In here, Granddad. We're going to be here for a while."

"Here, are we? Oh well, if you say so, then that's how it is—" He bowed to Mrs. Redmond. "There you are," he said. "After you, my dear." He took off his beret and began to turn it around restlessly.

Cleo, released from Ted's grasp, slunk on her belly

into the living room, fur standing brushlike away from her lithe, spotted body, nose wrinkling suspiciously.

Maureen bit her lip and looked about with an air of misery. "I'm awfully sorry about all this, Mrs. Redmond," she said. "It's—we're sort of a funny family, I'm afraid—"

"We invited you, remember?"

"I know, but—"

"We'll have fun," said Mrs. Redmond.

"I brought some kitty litter for Cleo. She's very well trained and—"

"Do stop worrying, Maureen," said Mrs. Redmond. "We'll have fun. I remember, when I was a girl, how we all used to love the coming of a storm. We'd get the candles in wine bottles placed around the rooms and then hope the electricity would go out, so we could light them. I remember it so well," she said dreamily. "It was like a fairyland, the candles burning in different colored bottles, with the flames flickering a little because the wind always gets through chinks somehow, and we'd look through the windows at the waves tossing— Come and look out of the windows in the living room," she said, taking Maureen by one hand and Nora by the other.

The lanterns at the end of the dock gleamed and disappeared and gleamed again, splashing the night with light, being doused as the waves swept over pilings, shining again as the water dropped and ran along the

187

dock and over the sides. Rain drummed torrentially on the aluminum roof, and the wind cried and moaned in the dark.

"Isn't it beautiful?" said Mrs. Redmond. Maureen, visibly relaxing, breathed deeply and said yes, it was glorious. Nora, still sniffling, looked up at Mrs. Redmond and said, "I like you."

"Oh, good."

"But I don't like him," she said, pointing at Mr. Redmond.

"Not everyone's obliged to," he said, grinning at his wife. "Well, if we've got that settled, I'll telephone the zoo—phone working okay, Josh? Good—then I'll get in touch with your father, Maureen, tell him not to worry."

"He'll probably stay there," said Ted, "if he knows we're safe here." His tone implied, unconsciously perhaps, that his father might've stayed at the zoo in any case.

Josh, going upstairs to show Maureen and Nora to the guest room, told Ted that Kevin and Granddad could use his room. "And you and I can bunk down on sleeping bags in the living room, okay?"

"Sure, great. Boy, your folks are something else, aren't they?"

"Yeah, I guess they are."

"Wow, I sure hope the electricity goes out, don't you?"

188

"Huh?" said Josh absently. "Oh sure. I hope so."

He looked out his window at the wild, wet, turbulent night and thought that when you came right down to it, his parents really were something else. Sometimes.

The power did not fail them. It failed. After a dinner which Mrs. Redmond cooked hot, saving the ham and boiled eggs and cole slaw and potatoes and other food she'd put away in the event of being unable to use the stove later on, the lights dimmed, flared, darkened, and went out.

"Oh boy, oh boy," said Kevin. "Oh boy, isn't this keen? Can I help light the candles, please? Lemme, huh?"

Maureen started to refuse, then looked at Mrs. Redmond, who said she saw no reason why not, she was sure he'd be very careful. And he was, indeed, careful. He went from one bottle to the next, positioning himself with suitable exactness before striking a wooden match and applying it to each wick. Mr. Redmond lit two kerosene lamps.

"It is sort of like a fairyland, isn't it?" Maureen said, sighing. "I never could have imagined anything like this. Such a storm, or that it would be—wonderful, beautiful."

The rain drumming on the roof made her low voice nearly inaudible, but her pleasure and contentment were clear as she sat in a big chair, Cleo asleep on her lap, her gaze going from the storm in the night to the room filled with colored wine bottles glimmering in candlelight.

"Like a magic night," she said again later, when with Mr. Redmond holding a lamp and leading the way, all but Ted and Josh went upstairs.

"Well," the two boys heard Mr. Redmond say as they disappeared into their various rooms, "I am obliged to tell you all one unenchanted fact. With the power out and the waters this high, nobody is to flush the toilets. Sorry, but that's how it is."

It appeared that even so gross a flaw could not perturb Maureen. "Oh, that's all right, Mr. Redmond," Josh heard her say. "No one'll mind."

My mother will, thought Josh, but he sort of agreed with Maureen. We never should've got rid of that outhouse, he said to himself, but wondered how, on nights like this, his ancestors had made it out to the thing. Probably used what they used to call thunder mugs, he decided.

"You know what a thunder mug is?" he asked Ted as they settled on their sleeping bags on the living-room floor (it was too hot to get into them).

"No. What?"

"Chamber pot. In the olden days, when people had outhouses and didn't want to go out to the outhouse, they used these chamber pots and stuck them under the beds."

"Oh yeah. I guess I heard about them. Cleo, you can't lie on my stomach all night. You're too heavy."

"I think the whole system is pretty peculiar," Josh went on. "She can sleep on my stomach."

"Let's just let her wander. She'll settle someplace. What whole system?"

"People's systems. Animals' systems. Even clams, come to that. All this masticating stuff and then having to get rid of it. Seems to me something better could've been thought up."

"By who?"

"I dunno. Evolution. Or God."

"Which one do you believe in?" Ted asked, and it seemed a reasonable question, part of the dark, of the storm, of a night when the elements took man's power and made it measly.

"Both, I guess," said Josh. "My father doesn't believe in God, but then my father doesn't believe in much of anything, when you come right down to it. Except the end of the world—he believes in that, all right."

"Mine, too," said Ted. "It's funny," he went on, after a long silence during which Josh thought about God and how for some reason he couldn't explain he was pretty sure God was there, no matter what his father said. Maybe not overseeing things, exactly, but just there. The way the planets were, and the ocean. Just there. He'd begun to think Ted must've fallen asleep when the voice from the other sleeping bag said,

"What I can't figure out, with your father and mine, both of them expecting everything to go boom any minute, why aren't they—angry, or frightened, or trying to do something about it?"

"Maybe because they're old—older, I mean."

"Do you think the world's going to end?" asked Ted.

"No, I don't," Josh said firmly. "I got too many things to do. Like grow up."

"You figured what you're gonna do then?"

"Oh boy," said Josh with relish. He put his hands behind his head. "Just think of it. How'd you like to design a boat with me and sail around the world? Not a racing boat—some nice beamy craft that'll sail herself, and we'll just—just be."

"It's a deal."

They were quiet again for a while. The storm assailed the wooden house, which seemed now and then to tremble and then to brace itself. The house had stood where it now stood, on the ocean's lip, for sixty years, and for sixty years had braced itself against forays and fury from sea and sky, and had survived. Josh was calmly sure it would survive this time, too.

"We don't have storms like this in Ohio," said Ted. "Thunderstorms, and once in a while a tornado hits, and of course there's snowstorms—"

"That's what I'd like to see," Josh said. "I've never seen any snow in my life, except on TV. Dad says that with the climatic changes that are taking place—he says probably because of all our mucking around in space, but I don't know about that—anyway, he says next year he'll probably just have to take me to Tallahassee for us to be in a real blizzard. They had fifteen inches of snow last winter in *Georgia*."

"I'm gonna miss the snow next winter. Snowstorms are the greatest."

"What do you do, build forts and stuff? Snowmen?"

"Sure. But I'll tell you the best part—it's coming out of school into a snowstorm and making snowballs and pitching them at cars."

"Don't the drivers get mad at you?"

"Do they ever!" Ted hooted. "Some guys, even ladies, stop and get out and try to catch us, but by then we're gone, brother, long gone." He sighed happily, recalling chases and shouted curses through the falling snow. "It's wild."

"Would you like to move back to Ohio?"

Ted thought a long time. "Sort of. For one thing, I can't figure what we're gonna do with Granddad here. I mean, when school starts, and that's just around the corner. Dad—he just keeps putting off deciding anything, and Maureen and I can't figure it out. Up home —I mean in Ohio—my Aunt Ruth took care of Granddad during the day. She's my father's sister, but she can't just up and leave her family and all and come down here and take care of him. We keep telling Dad something's gotta be decided and he says sure, sure and doesn't decide. He's crazy about Granddad, you know, but Maureen and I think he's better at making arrangements for animals than for—well, people. Us, like. When the time comes for Cleo to be arranged for, when she's too big for us to keep—well, she'll be *arranged* for. But Granddad—" Ted sighed, yawned. "Well, it'll work out."

Ted had never talked like this before. And that, too, Josh thought, was somehow part of the storm. There was something about storms that made people, his father said, drop their normal barriers, say things they normally wouldn't say, do things they wouldn't think of doing on a calm day, or even just a plain rainy or windy one.

Everything got released in a storm like this. Boats lost their moorings, people lost their tempers; walls were loosened, and tongues. That was what Mr. Redmond said. Josh started to tell Ted about his father's theory and how he thought it was right, but as he opened his mouth a soft jerky snore came from the other bag.

Josh stayed awake a little longer.

Now and then, through the screaming of the wind, the pelting and pummeling of the rain on the roof, the crashing and thudding of waves against the dock and on the beach, he could make out the wail of sirens, and he thought that perhaps they were taking people away from the Gulf side of the island, evacuating that side, and maybe even this.

194

But down here at Lands End they would ride it out, as they always had before. As they always would.

He smiled drowsily as a furry, purring body snuggled up to his. Cleo pushed her head until she had it snugly pressed under his arm. Her tail flopped a few times, hitting his doubled-up knees. Then she fell asleep, and so did he.

16

Hank Burroughs returned from Massachusetts the week-end before school started, and one of the first things he did was ride around to see how old Josh had made out during the summer. He found him on the dock in the sun, lounging in the old redwood chair with a mug of coffee beside him and the *Encyclopædia Britannica* in his lap.

"Still at it, huh?" said Hank, sitting down and leaning over to study the pilings. "Boy, one day this whole thing's gonna go. Looks like it took a helluva beating in the storm."

"It stood. The whole island took a beating."

"So I hear. And see. Our house is okay." Hank peered at the volume in Josh's hand. "Still on Diphtheria? You take a course in slow reading or something?"

"I've got past Diplodocus. He was an eighty-foot dinosaur, but he only gets five lines here. Now comes Diplomacy. That should be pretty good, I figure."

"But you didn't read it all summer, did you? Whatcha been doin'?"

Josh shrugged, and then as Hank went on looking as if he was actually interested, added, "Mostly I spent the time with the Arthurs."

"That vet's family? My mother says they up and went back to Ohio after the storm, and now Dr. Claven's having to do the whole job himself again. They sure don't have much luck with their vets over there, do they?"

"Dr. Arthur is a swell vet."

"Okay, okay. I didn't say he wasn't. But a swell vet in Ohio isn't doing our zoo much good, is he?"

"They had to go back, especially after Tincture of— Did you come past their old house coming here?"

"Wow, did I! Looks like the wreck of the Hesperus. What was the Hesperus, Josh?"

"A boat."

"That's what I thought. That old hulk of a house looks sort of like a boat wreck, doesn't it? One of the town engineers was over there a while ago, and he told me they're going to take it down. Take what's left down. It's a danger to the community, he says."

The storm that night had savaged the air and the land until early morning, and then seemed to fold over

197

on itself and subside, in the way of tropical storms. When the Redmonds and the Arthurs came out of the house a little before dawn to see what had been wrecked, they found the bay waters still high, but moving indolently. Pine branches and palm fronds were strewn everywhere, and the traveler's palm where the mockingbirds loved to perch was lying on its side, shallow roots straggling about it pitifully. The boats were safe, the dock still stood, the birds were once again about their ceaseless search for food.

The sun, a tremendous orange ball, lifted rapidly into the sky, daubed the waters, the wet trees, the swept and sparkling sands with dawn.

Dr. Arthur, stubble-bearded, blinking with fatigue, drove up in the van and got out. "I don't know how to thank you," he said to Mr. and Mrs. Redmond. "I just don't know what to say."

"You could say how you like your eggs and how you take your coffee," Mrs. Redmond suggested. "The power is on again, and we're all hungry and I imagine you are."

"Am I," he said, yawning. "But really, you'll never know how grateful I am for what you did. I couldn't get away from the zoo—actually literally couldn't, after a certain point, and before that we were so busy seeing to the animals that I didn't take in how bad things were going to get. I guess maybe we'd better go over and see how the house fared—"

"Not until you've eaten," said Mrs. Redmond. "Then we'll all go."

At the other side of the island the Gulf waters came into shore in long low rollers topped with froth, so gentle-seeming that even the Redmonds, accustomed to the moody sea, were unprepared for what it had done to Tincture of Spain.

When they rounded the curve in the road and the house came into view, Ted, who was riding with them, stared and rubbed his eyes and said shakily, "What *is* that? What *happened*?"

What had been a house—certainly in need of repair, but still a house with walls and windows and a roof—had overnight gone, too far for reclamation, toward following the house that had stood in front of it many years before and now was just a few foundation stones starting up from the waters when the tide was low.

The entire wall facing the Gulf had collapsed and the seas had poured in, bringing tons of sand and shells and crustaceans that piled against the inside walls, crushing them, bringing the staircase down, breaking the furniture and tossing the pieces like flotsam. All that remained, in fact, of Tincture of Spain, were three outside walls that might go at any time, and the great center ceiling beam from which Senator Freebee had dangled long ago and from which part of Cleo's crib now dangled instead.

The van, which had arrived before them, was pulled up next to the iron gate, torn from its hinges and now blocking entry to the driveway. Dr. Arthur was out, standing with his fists doubled against his head, like someone trying to make himself wake up. Nora was screaming, leaning against Maureen, who absently patted her shoulder and said, "There, there," in a dazed and dreamy tone. Kevin came rushing over to the Redmonds shouting "Hey, lookit. Lookit what happened. Lookit our house!"

"I can't believe it," Mrs. Redmond said. She went over to Dr. Arthur and looked at him closely. "Are you all right?"

For a moment he didn't answer. Then he looked at her, at Mr. Redmond, at his children, his father, and back to the house. "My God," he said. "My *God*." His voice was soft and shaky. "Suppose they'd *been* here?"

"Well, they weren't," said Mrs. Redmond. "We don't have to—"

"They might have been. I left them here. I didn't realize—I didn't know—"

"Of course you didn't," said Mrs. Redmond. "How could you? You've never been in a storm like this. In fact, this is the worst we've had in—in years. And at that, the hurricane didn't actually hit us, you know."

"Didn't *hit* us!" Dr. Arthur began to laugh. He leaned on the hood of the van, his shoulders shaking. "Didn't hit us—that's rich!"

"Well, it didn't," Mrs. Redmond said, putting a tentative hand on his arm, at which he straightened and stopped laughing. "It missed the island and hit about fifty or sixty miles north of here. We got the report on the radio earlier."

"What kind of place *is* this—" he began, then shrugged and shuddered. "I feel as if I were in hell. I almost lost my whole family, and if it hadn't been for you—" Rubbing his hand roughly across his face, he took a heavy breath and opened the door of the van, where his father was still sitting and Cleo was clambering around, mewing to be let out.

"Let's go home," said old Mr. Arthur to his son. "That's the ticket. Let's you and me go home."

"Okay, Pop," said Dr. Arthur. "That's just exactly what we're going to do. Go home."

"You'll come and stay with us," said Mrs. Redmond. "Until you can get resettled. We'll manage nicely—"

"No. No, thank you very very much, dear Mrs. Redmond. And thank you, Mr. Redmond. For my family's life. And you, too, Josh, of course. The three of you undoubtedly saved them, and beyond saying thank you I don't know what to say, except that I'll be—be grateful to you—all the rest of my life. But it's all—" He closed his eyes briefly, and clenched his teeth. "It's too much, and I can't take it here."

"What will you—what do you plan to do?"

"I have a friend at home who wants me to go into

practice with him, and that's what we're going to do, Pop and the kids and I. We're going back to Ohio and make some money."

"We *are*?" Maureen cried out. She flung her arms around her father, her face alive with joy. "We really truly are?"

"We are."

"Well, but when—" Mrs. Redmond began. "You can't just go now, just like that."

"Oh, yes we can," said Dr. Arthur. "We can, and we're going to. We're going now, this minute," he told them all grimly. "We're going to get in this van and drop Cleo at the zoo and just keep on driving."

Ted and Josh stared at each other, speechless, while Mr. Redmond, shocked into speech, said, "But Dr. Arthur—that's impossible."

"Why? We hardly need to pack up, do we?" He waved a hand at what had been his house. "We'd need a bulldozer to find anything, if we could use it when we found it."

"But what about the zoo? What about Dr. Claven? What will he do—"

"I've been telling Dr. Claven for weeks that I cannot support my family on what they're paying—"

"You must have known what the pay was going to be before you came."

"I didn't know that the price of everything was going to double in a few months, and I didn't realize they wouldn't listen to a reasonable request for an increase, and I didn't realize that my family was going to hate this place and be endangered by it—"

"I don't hate it," Ted began, but stopped when Kevin and Nora and Maureen all began to shout at once that they wanted to go home and he wasn't going to stop them.

"I scarcely know what to say," Mrs. Redmond said faintly. "It's so—so abrupt, your decision."

"Well, it isn't, not really," Dr. Arthur said. "I've been half thinking about it for some time. Since I asked for a raise and was told it was out of the question. And there's the matter of what to do with my father. I just can't—can't manage here. I never should have come. No, we're going. Now."

"Well, please," said Mrs. Redmond. "At least come home with us and let me pack some food for you to take on the trip. We have so much that I prepared against the storm, you know. It would be a favor if you'd take some of it. And perhaps we can find a few changes of clothes for the children. Maybe Maureen could use something of mine, and I probably have stuff stored somewhere that Josh used when he was younger that Kevin could use, and Ted, too. Then you'd only have to stop and get Nora something—"

"You're too kind," said Dr. Arthur wearily. "We accept, of course." But he didn't sound pleased, only grateful, and in less than an hour Josh heard, for the last time, the rattling of the old VW van as Dr. Arthur headed for the zoo, to hand in his notice and hand over Cleo.

"That's the most irresponsible, the most in*cred*ible man," said Mrs. Redmond when they'd gone, "that I have ever in my lifetime heard of. I know five-year-old children with more sense of responsibility. I can't believe him."

"I don't believe it yet," said Mr. Redmond. "The man's—he's—people just don't *do* things like that."

They both looked at Josh then, expecting perhaps that he'd defend the Arthurs. But he didn't. He said nothing. Not a thing. He went up to his room and sat on the window seat and thought that it was funny, people talked about hearts and how they could ache, but he'd never realized before that a heart actually could hurt, as if someone had punched it.

He'd loved the Arthurs. Ted and old Mr. Arthur especially, but all of them, that family in that house. He'd loved them and needed them and now they were gone.

Dr. Arthur had said that he'd have to come up to Ohio and visit them. "In the winter, when it's snowing," he'd said. "You come up sometime and spend a couple of weeks with us."

Well, maybe he'd do that. Maybe. If he did, it wouldn't be the same, in no way would it be the same as it had been here. But maybe he'd go. Sometime.

"It's peculiar," Mrs. Redmond said that night at dinner, "how out of all of it, the storm, and meeting the family at last and watching them take off in that unheard-of way, the one I most remember is old Mr. Arthur. Those floating sentences. And the perfect manners. How strange, really, to find that courtesy endures when the rest of the mind is in tatters."

"I wonder where they are now," Mr. Redmond said, and glanced at Josh, who didn't speak. All through dinner Josh remained with his elbows on the table, chin on his hands, not speaking and not eating. And his parents didn't ask him either to remove his elbows or to get on with his dinner. They just looked at him from time to time and went on talking to each other, and to him, as if he were answering.

But the days went by, and gradually the feeling of having lost something he couldn't do without began to lessen, and one day he went over to the zoo to see Cleo. It was awful how, if you'd been to a place with people you liked and then went back there without them, it seemed empty and horribly sad. But he couldn't stop going places because the Arthurs weren't around anymore. That'd mean he couldn't go much of anyplace around here, and around here was the only place he could go.

He'd gone to see Cleo because she was now the zoo's female jaguar. Fatima, one night, had given up her bitter ghost. Clara had found her in the morning, stiff and cold, lips curled back to show her teeth in a snarl, her parting comment to the world. As the zoo had no other female jaguar, they'd decided to keep Cleo. And every day, when Josh went to see her, she ran forward to greet him at the bars of her cage. In the evening, when the zoo was closed, Clara still let him go into the cage and play with the little jaguar who was just this side of not being little anymore.

"She'll go on being friendly," Clara had said to him yesterday, "and chances are she'll always recognize you and want to play with you; but pretty soon her friendship will be the kind that would leave you scattered around the cage in several pieces. I think you're better all in one piece," she'd added, smiling.

Josh had looked up at her. She was a tall girl, and friendly, and sort of nice-looking.

"You miss them?" he'd asked, surprising himself. "The Arthurs, I mean?"

"I know who you meant." Clara caught her lower lip briefly with her teeth, then she gave a sighing kind of laugh. "Sure I do, Josh. They were—are—a lovely family. Kind of unpredictable, or do I mean unreliable, but—" She turned away. "Have to get back to the office, get caught up on the files. Dr. Claven can't do everything. He tries, of course."

"They gonna get a new vet?"

"Dr. Claven's going to interview some. This time, he says, he's going to get somebody right out of veterinary school, somebody without a family. Without even a wife, he says." Josh thought she'd brightened a little at that, but he couldn't be sure and didn't really care.

He just hoped he'd be able to play with Cleo for a while yet, and he hoped she would remember him after he couldn't go into the cage anymore.

"Hey, man—what's happened to you?" Hank said. He sounded as if he'd said it a couple of times already.

"What d'ya mean, what's happened? Nothing's happened."

"Nothing's happened? You sit there not saying a word for—it's been fifteen minutes since you opened your trap. Something *must've* happened. Last I saw you, nobody could get a word in edgewise."

Josh closed the *Encyclopædia Britannica* (Daisy to Educational) and took a sip of his coffee. "People don't always just stay the same, you know. People change. Or if they don't, they ought to."

"You mean me? What am I supposed to change, huh?"

"I can't think of anything if you can't."

Hank stood up. "Boy, you're some cheery party to greet after a summer away. See you around, maybe," he added, stamping off down the dock.

Josh looked after him, scratching his head. One thing that sure didn't change was the way he and Hank got along. Or didn't get along. Either way, it came out to sort of the same thing, this sort of friendship the two of them had had practically since they were born. They'd see each other around, and no maybe.

207

But you didn't say to a guy like Hank that you'd quit talking so much because you'd decided to do some thinking, and some listening. It'd sound sort of dumb or stuck-up, said to Hank.

He looked out over the bay, where pelicans were diving, accompanied by their tormentors, the gulls. The tide was going out, and with it a line of porpoises arching and sliding through the waves. The sun glinted on their sharklike fins and their whalelike flukes as they curved upward, disappeared, reappeared, going out of the pass to the Gulf.

He guessed he'd take *Scorch* and go over to Catfish Island. It'd be sort of lonely without Ted, but just the same he was going. By the time he got there the tide would be out enough so that he could lie on the flats and let the little fish nibble at him. He'd get on with his thinking. And, just in case the thinking didn't go too well, he'd take along his rod and do some casting.

In any case, he was going out on *Scorch*, by himself. He went down the dock to get the mast and centerboard. The sky was blue, the waters green, the wind was southwest and steady, and he guessed he wouldn't ask for more.

Format by Kohar Alexanian
Set in 12 pt. Janson
Composed and bound by The Haddon Craftsmen, Inc.
Printed by The Murray Printing Co.
HARPER & ROW, PUBLISHERS, INCORPORATED